No Big Deal

No Big Deal

Ellen Jaffe McClain

Lodestar Books

DUTTON   NEW YORK

for Spencer,
who irons,
and in memory of my grandmother,
Rose G. Roth,
who knows

Copyright © 1994 by Ellen Jaffe McClain

Library of Congress Cataloging-in-Publication Data

McClain, Ellen Jaffe.
  No big deal/Ellen Jaffe McClain.—1st ed.
    p. cm.
  Summary: When rumors that Janice's favorite teacher is gay begin to circulate at school and in the community, she decides to stand up for him even in the face of her mother's opposition.
  ISBN 0-525-67483-7
  [1. Homosexuality—Fiction. 2. Teacher-student relationships—Fiction. 3. High schools—Fiction. 4. Schools—Fiction. 5. Mothers and daughters—Fiction.] I. Title.
  PZ7.M47841365No 1994
  [Fic]—dc20   94-2580
                                                              CIP
                                                               AC

Published in the United States by Lodestar Books, .
an affiliate of Dutton Children's Books,
a division of Penguin Books USA Inc.,
375 Hudson Street, New York, New York 10014

Published simultaneously in Canada
by McClelland & Stewart, Toronto

Editor: Rosemary Brosnan
Designer: Marilyn Granald

Printed in the U.S.A.   First Edition
10 9 8 7 6 5 4 3 2 1

❧ 1 ❧

"Hey, Huey!"

Ignore him.

"Yo, Baby Huey!" boomed The Voice from the back of the bus.

This is really getting old, I thought, as a bunch of future hamburger-flippers giggled in appreciation of Kevin Lynch's so-called wit.

Just ignore him. Read your book.

I sat in my usual seat, two behind the driver, and pulled *A Tree Grows in Brooklyn* out of my backpack. Why didn't anyone ever rag on Kevin? He's one of the fattest guys in the ninth grade. Of course he's also one of the tallest guys in ninth grade. I'd never actually seen him beat up anybody, but he certainly looks like he could.

Forget him, Janice. Read the book so you can give it back to Mr. P.

Two-ton. Lardass. Gargantua. Where does someone his size get off calling me Baby Huey? Next time I should just say, "What is it, Your Blubberosity?"

He'd just laugh and call you something worse.

It was freezing outside for November, but warm enough on the school bus to make my glasses fog up. I unwound my scarf and wondered how big a crater Kevin would make in the sidewalk if I threw him off a twenty-story building.

Fifteen minutes later I was far away, in fact I was somewhere in Brooklyn around 1917, when I heard The Voice again, not booming this time, but as a high-pitched whisper uncomfortably close to my right ear. " 'I will tell you the truth as a woman,' " it said, reading over my shoulder. " 'It would have been a very beautiful thing. Because there is only once that you love that way.' Aren't you a little young to be reading porno, Huey?"

"It's a classic, buttbrain," I said, showing Kevin the cover.

He grabbed the book from me. "A young girl's coming of age," he read. "I don't think so, Huey. You're just not mature enough for this kind of literature."

"Give it back, I borrowed it from Mr. Padovano," I said, turning around and reaching for it.

"No way, Tutti-Frutti Padovano's only interested in young *boys,*" Kevin said cracking himself up.

"He is not. Give it back," I said. Kevin held the book out of reach. I knew he wouldn't give it back as long as I tried to grab it, but I was scared he'd throw it to one of those idiots in the back of the bus. When Mr. P gave it to me, he told me it was his sister's, that when he started teaching, he'd gone through all the books they'd had as kids and taken the ones he thought his students would like too.

2

The guys in the back weren't looking at Kevin, though, and when I didn't hear "Hey, guys, catch!" I turned around and stared out the window, watching the last few leaves fall off the trees. As the bus stopped in front of the school, Kevin bopped me on the head with the book and dropped it in my lap. "Have a nice day, Huey," he said. "Be sure to give Tutti-Frutti a big, sloppy, wet one from me." He made a disgusting kissing noise as he stomped off the bus, rocking it with every step.

I got off next. "Bye, Baby Huey!" the creeps in back chorused.

About ten feet, I decided. The crater Kevin made would be ten feet wide and five feet deep, and windows would shatter for blocks around.

"Come on, class," Ms. Zaiman pleaded. "How many square feet bigger would each wall be if the rooms were divided on the diagonal? Answer to the nearest hundredth."

Eighty-nine point forty-six, I thought, ordering myself not to raise my hand. I'd already raised it about twelve times and been called on at least eight. God, somebody else must have it by now. I stopped staring at the four-sided pyramid on the chalkboard and looked around the room. A few kids were still asleep, halfway through period one. Most of the rest were drawing pictures, passing notes, or doing homework. A couple were poking at their calculators, but at the rate they were going, it would take the rest of the period. We'd already spent fifteen minutes on this one word problem. I couldn't stand it anymore. I raised my hand.

About ten kids groaned softly. Ms. Zaiman looked annoyed. "Someone who is not named Janice Green, please," she said. I put my hand down. She says that almost every day. "Class, I'm sure someone other than Janice can figure this out." Skippy Isserman raised his hand. "Good—Skippy," she said.

"A hundred and seventy-eight point ninety-two," he said.

"No, but you're on the right track," Ms. Zaiman said encouragingly. "Try again." Skippy shook his head and turned back to his calculator. "Anyone else?" she said. She glanced at the clock, then at me. "All right, Janice," she said sourly.

"Eighty-nine point forty-six?" I said, trying to sound like I wasn't sure. The class buzzed anyway as Ms. Zaiman wrote *89.46 sq. ft.* on the board. "Huey, nine, Zaiman, zip," whispered Jimmy De Milio, two seats behind me, as Ms. Zaiman reminded Skippy that he had forgotten to divide by two. "Thank you, Janice," Heather Rubin said under her breath in a singsongy voice.

"Thank you, Janice," Ms. Zaiman said.

Okay, I raise my hand too much. What am I supposed to do, just sit there and give Ms. Zaiman a blank stare like everybody else does? The class is boring enough as it is. At least I don't *wave* it anymore. I used to practically throw myself out of my chair. One day in seventh grade I was leaning forward, trying to get called on, and the kid behind me reached over and pulled my chair so the desk attached to it hit me in the stomach. Since then I sit quietly and raise my hand about halfway.

4

"So we *finally* find out that a wall constructed on the diagonal would be eighty-nine point forty-six square feet larger than one built parallel to the edge of the pyramid," Ms. Zaiman said. "Janice, would you go through the problem for us on the chalkboard?"

Ms. Zaiman was wearing a black sweater and skirt. Forget it. I'm not doing your job just 'cause you don't want to get chalk dust all over you. I hate going up to the chalkboard, especially in math. Ms. Zaiman is short and slender, and standing by the board, I always feel like King Kong. "No, that's okay," I said.

"It is not okay," she replied. "I want all the steps on the board, and you seem to be the only student with her brain plugged in this morning. Come on." She held out the chalk. Most of the kids started to chant, "Janice, Janice."

Just then a student runner from one of the offices came in and handed Ms. Zaiman a summons. "Looks like you're spared, Janice," she said. "You're wanted in the guidance office."

A few kids went "Ooooooooooh," as if I were in trouble. I got up and headed to the front of the room. "Take your stuff," the runner said. Another "Ooooooooooh." What a bunch of bozos. It was the guidance office, not the assistant principal's. I got my books and followed the runner into the hall.

The secretary in the guidance office said Ms. Hoxley, the ninth-grade counselor, wanted to see me, so I stood by her doorway. She was talking on the phone. Some girl I'd never seen before was sitting in the chair next to her desk. She was really pretty, with long blonde hair pulled back in a barrette. She wore a pink sweater and skirt right out of *Seventeen* magazine. Total drill-team look, but she didn't have the nose-in-the-air, I'm-so-cool expression the drill-team types always have. She kept her eyes down and looked sort of shy. Ms. Hoxley got off the phone, wrote something on a card, and gave it to the blonde girl.

"Okay, you're all set," she said. Then she looked up and saw me. "Oh, hi, Janice. This is Holly Johansen. She just moved here from upstate. Would you take her around today? She has almost all the same classes you do. Holly, this is Janice Green."

"Hi," I said.

"Hi," Holly said, getting up. She had huge blue eyes and was a head shorter than I was. I wanted to hate her, but she seemed very nice.

"Have Ms. Zaiman sign her in before the bell rings," Ms. Hoxley said.

"Okay, sure. Come on, we only have a few minutes before period one is over," I said to Holly.

"Thank you, Ms. Hoxley," Holly said politely.

"You must be honors if we have the same classes," I said in the hall. "Lemme see your program." She handed me the card. "Yeah, it's all the same, except I have Spanish and you have French."

"My parents wanted me to take Spanish, but I have this dream of living in Paris someday," Holly said.

"Cool," I said. "Well, you must be reasonably smart if they put you in honors everything without an argument."

"They *did* put up an argument," Holly said. "The counselor called my old school. They don't have separate honors classes there, but my mom brought me in and she told the counselor that I've been taking geometry and biology and I need to be in honors classes if you had them here. Then she had to go to work. They must be really careful about who gets into honors here."

I snorted. "Oh, sure, you have to be Albert Einstein," I said sarcastically. "That's just the way they do things. See, West River has this reputation for having really great schools, so they never want to admit that anybody coming in from another district could possibly keep up. Half the kids I know are in honors, and a lot of them aren't so brilliant. You really must be smart if they took your old school's word for it."

"Oh, not really," Holly said modestly.

"Well, don't worry, I don't think anything's gonna be too hard for you," I said. "And I'll show you around. We're even in the same homeroom."

"Thanks," Holly said. "I was afraid I'd have to find everything myself. This school is humongous compared to the one I was going to." Definitely not a drill-team type.

Ms. Zaiman signed Holly's program card, and we went to homeroom, since the bell was about to ring. "After announcements we're supposed to read silently for like ten minutes," I told Holly. "The teacher usually has stuff lying around if you don't have anything."

"I've got the first section of the *Times*," Holly said. "My mom reads it early and gives it to me before she leaves for work."

"You get the *New York Times?* Every day?" We only get it on Sunday.

7

"Uh-huh."

"What does your mom do?" I asked.

"She's an editor in a publishing house. She used to be a freelance editor, but when she told them we were moving down here, they offered her a job in their office."

"Why'd you move here from upstate?"

"My dad's a real estate developer. He built a lot of houses where we used to live, and now he's building town houses down here. They picked West River for us to live in 'cause it's supposed to have good schools."

"You got any brothers or sisters?"

"You ask a lot of questions," Holly said, smiling.

"I'm sorry," I said. "People are always telling me that."

"I don't mind," she said. "I have a little brother. Do you have any sisters or brothers?"

"I have a sister in fifth grade."

We kept walking down the long hall. Lockers, cinder blocks, doors, lockers, cinder blocks, doors. Holly looked like she was thinking of a question to ask me. "What are you going to read in homeroom?" she asked finally.

"*A Tree Grows in Brooklyn,*" I said. "I only have ten pages to go."

"I read that last year! I love it," Holly said.

"Yeah, it's great," I said. "I like books where people find out about life."

"I do too," Holly said. Her little *Seventeen* skirt swished from side to side. I couldn't believe I was talking about books with someone who looked like half a Doublemint commercial.

"I read this book a few months ago called *The Heart Is a Lonely Hunter*," I said. "It's sort of the same kind of thing, only the girl is a little older and it's in the South."

"Wasn't that a movie?"

"Yeah, I saw the movie on TV and it was really good, so I read the book."

"Have you read anything by Ursula Le Guin?" Holly asked.

"No, who's she?"

"She writes science fiction, mostly," Holly said. "I read a lot of science fiction. Everybody at my old school thought I was weird."

I looked at her, a strange, happy feeling blooming in my head. "I don't think you're weird."

Holly smiled up at me. "Good," she said.

❧ 2 ❧

*E*verything I learned about Holly that morning was good news. She was shy with people, but not too shy to raise her hand, and fifteen minutes into biology class I realized she was going to take a lot of pressure off me as West River Junior High's number-one ninth-grade female nerd. And she could get away with it, too, because she was cute, and unlike me, she only raised her hand about every third question. But you could tell that she knew every single answer.

I figured Holly would lose interest in being my friend after seeing what a spazo blimp I am in P.E. But luckily we were playing volleyball, the one sport I can almost play like a normal human being because I'm so tall and I'm very careful always to hit the ball with both hands. Once I got a good shot over the net and Holly yelled, "All right, Janice!" Then the next time I served, I got the ball really low, just clearing the net, and the other side couldn't return it, and one of the *boys* on our team said, "Good serve." I got to make the next five serves.

Between classes Holly told me that she and her family had been living in this really small town, and her mom had taught part-time in the state college at Oneonta. And I thought West River was far from the city! It takes my dad about an hour to drive into New York every day. Holly said it takes *five* hours to get there from where she used to live. She's only been to New York twice in her whole life. We go at least every couple of months to visit relatives or see a play. New York's a lot more interesting than West River, and when my parents let me hang out there by myself, I'm gonna go all the time. From what Holly said, upstate's even more boring than West River. Her old town was so small that they had the junior and senior high schools in the same building!

Kevin came up behind me in the cafeteria and took the ice cream cup off my tray just as Holly and I came off the lunch line. "Uh-uh-uh, gotta watch those calories, Huey," he said.

Usually I'd just grab back whatever he took and move on, but I was still feeling good about the volleyball game. "If I were you, I'd do a few thousand sit-ups before I made comments about anybody else's size," I said.

For a split second, Kevin flashed me an angry look, like I'd actually hurt his feelings. Then he laughed. "Aw, this is just the end of my baby fat," he said. "You're lookin' at raw, lean muscle."

"Yeah, right," I said disgustedly. "Come on, Holly."

"Wait up," Kevin said, pulling on my sweater. "Who's your little friend?"

"Let go!" I said. "Nobody who wants to know *you*."

I marched off fast, Holly behind me, and we found a couple of places to sit at the end of a table.

"What was *that?*" Holly asked, referring to Kevin. She looked as disgusted as I was, especially when she saw him pick up someone's left-behind sandwich from a tray and start eating it.

"Kevin Lynch, also known as The Thing That Ate West River," I said. We watched him go around the cafeteria, bellowing greetings at people who mostly tried to ignore him. He slapped one kid on the back and almost pushed his face into his spaghetti and meatballs.

"He looks like an awful bully," Holly said.

"Not really," I said. "I mean, he doesn't beat up smaller kids or take their lunch money. I guess he's kind of a verbal bully. He says really rude things to people sometimes, and mostly they just take it, I guess because he *could* beat 'em up if he wanted to."

"What did he call you before?" Holly asked.

"Huey, like Baby Huey, you know, from the comic book," I said, my face getting hot.

"I don't read comic books," Holly said. "Is that some kind of animal?"

"Yeah, a duck dressed like a baby," I said. Baby Huey is in fact a huge, pear-shaped, potbellied, goofy-looking duck wearing a baby bonnet and a diaper, but I didn't see any reason to tell Holly that. "It's not just 'cause of how I look, it's also that I'm like the youngest in the class," I continued.

"How old are you?"

"I'm still thirteen. I won't be fourteen until the end of December."

"You're only thirteen?" Holly said. She sounded

shocked. "I'll be fifteen in January." Well, so much for Holly being my friend. She probably thinks I'm a big baby. "I thought you were older."

"Yeah, everybody does at first, because I'm tall," I said.

"Well, that, and you're really smart, and you just act older than thirteen," Holly said. That made me feel good. Usually nobody accuses me of acting very mature. "Do a lot of kids call you Baby Huey?" she asked.

Uh-oh. I could say, no, just Kevin, but then she'd hear someone else say it and I'd be a liar. "Not so much anymore," I said. "Kevin started it in sixth grade, when we were in the same class. He got *everybody* calling me Huey. And they kept it up in seventh grade, but after that it wasn't so bad. Now it's just a few of the boys who know me from elementary. Especially Kevin."

"Well, I think that sucks," Holly said. I started laughing and almost choked on a bite of salad. I didn't expect someone as ladylike as Holly looked to use the word *sucks*. "And I think Kevin's really gross."

"Oh, he doesn't bother me much anymore," I said. "He's just an unpleasant fact of life, like going to the dentist."

Every so often one of the really popular ninth-grade girls—and a couple of the guys—would cruise by where we were sitting and get a good look at Holly. "Why are people staring at me?" she finally asked.

"You're new." I shrugged. "Plus you look real drill-team, so they can't figure out why you're sitting with me."

"Don't you usually sit with anyone at lunch?"

"Sometimes, with kids who used to go to Hebrew school with me. Like Sheila Mikulsky over there," I said, pointing discreetly, "and Rachel Strauss. You saw them earlier; they're in our classes."

"You went to Hebrew school?" Holly asked.

"Yeah, for three years. I'm still going to religious school."

"Did you have a what-do-you-call-it?"

"A bat mitzvah? Sure, last winter," I said. "Weren't there any Jewish kids at your old school?"

"I don't think so."

"Boy, you're in for a change. Half the kids in West River are Jewish. We have two temples, and they're both big. Most of the kids here belong to a youth group in their temple or church."

"We've never belonged to a church," Holly said. "How do you get to know people in a school this humongous?"

"Don't think of it as humongous," I said. "It's more like a bunch of little schools shoved together. We have classes with mostly the same kids all day. Those are the kids you're gonna get to know, plus anyone you meet in activities or things you do outside of school."

"What did you mean, I look drill-team?" Holly asked.

"Well, you have really nice long hair, and you're really pretty"—Holly went all red—"and you're wearing great clothes, and that's their look," I said. "They're all sitting over there. See what I mean?"

Holly glanced over her shoulder. "I guess," she said. "I didn't want to wear these clothes. Usually I just wear

14

jeans to school, but my mother made me dress up for the first day."

"You don't have to apologize," I said. "But that's why some of them were staring at you. Around here, the way you look says what clique you're in, and right now you look like part of that whole drill-team, student-council, golden-girl crowd."

"But I'm not like that at all," Holly said. "I hate girls like that."

"Then you should probably wear jeans tomorrow. Otherwise they'll start circling in closer." I put on a snobby voice. " 'Hi, your name's Holly, right? Wanna sit with us? We're really cool.' "

Holly laughed and looked around the room. "I can see what you mean about cliques," she said.

"Oh, it's terrible," I said, pointing again. "My favorite is the science-nerd table. If a girl, any girl, goes over there and talks to one of them, they all look at her like she's a hostile life form from another galaxy. Then the Asian kids sit there, and *they're* divided into the ones who were born here and the ones who are still learning English, except for Felicia Rim, who sits with the student council, and the hard-core heavy-metal types sit over there by the restrooms, and so on and so forth."

"And you don't belong to a clique?" Holly asked.

"Not really," I said. "I'm sort of classified under Miscellaneous Nerds. Sometimes people talk to me during lunch, like about some assignment we're all working on, and sometimes I just read. Sometimes I wind up at a whole table of nerds who aren't real social, and we all sit there reading."

"I guess I'm a Miscellaneous Nerd too," Holly said.

The bell rang and everybody started throwing away trash and heading out. "Is it period five now?" Holly asked.

"No, this is activity period," I said. "They don't have a lot of stuff after school because everybody has to race off to piano lessons and ice hockey and orthodontia and like that, so they put all the extracurricular activities after lunch. You can do the same thing every day or break it up. I work in school publications twice a week and tutor twice a week, and Fridays I help with recycling. There's a chorus, and an orchestra, and an art program, and a science club. And sports."

"Is there a computer lab here?"

"Oh, sure, it's always open this period. It's like all science nerds, so don't expect to make a lot of friends there." I took Holly to the computer lab, which made her eyes light up—our school district is short on imagination but long on hardware—and told her I'd pick her up for English class at the end of the period.

On the way to class I gave her a new spiral notebook. "You'll need this for English," I said. "Mr. Geiger is like eighty years old, and you have to do everything his way, which means spiral notebook, headings centered at the top of the page, blue or black ink, and when he gives page thirty-five of notes, you write thirty-five in numbers no bigger than one-quarter inch high in the upper right-hand corner of the page."

"Gee, he sounds like lots of fun," Holly said.

"Everything's grammar; we hardly ever read," I said. "He says nothing worth reading's been written since 1940, and our minds aren't developed enough to read what's good, but he can by God teach us sentence structure. It's an easy A if you don't die from an overdose of worksheets. But if you make it through the period, you get Mr. P as a reward."

"He must be wonderful; you mentioned him before," Holly said. "Does he do magic tricks or something?"

"Almost," I said. "You'll see."

3

Mr. Padovano's the best teacher I ever had, that's all. It's not just that he's really good-looking, and nice without being a pushover, and knows a lot, although that's all true. It's the way he teaches. Ninth-grade social studies is world geography, and for most teachers, that means memorizing lists of rivers and religions and principal products, filling out worksheets for homework, and barfing it all back on tests.

But Mr. P isn't satisfied with that. He announced the first week of school that we're all smart enough to get the facts from the textbook, and his job was to make us *think*. I mean, he deals with maps and charts and lists, but he goes way further. He says world geography is always changing, and we can't keep up with it out of a textbook. So he makes us read the newspaper at least once a week and is forever handing out articles that have to do with stuff we're learning. He knows people from all over the world. In two months we've already had three guest speakers.

Mostly he wants us to think about what he calls the what-ifs. What if the English hadn't colonized any of America? What if Muhammad hadn't founded Islam? What if the Africans had been able to keep the slave traders from taking them away? When you think about questions like that, you see how the world could have turned out really different; our own lives could be really different right now. Even the lazy kids get involved in the discussions we wind up having when Mr. P throws a what-if at us.

Holly's first class with Mr. P was typical, which means it was really interesting. We were studying world patterns of migration, like the Native Americans originally coming from Asia across the Bering Strait when there was still land there, and after some review, he started a discussion about how and why individuals migrate.

"Migration can change almost everything about you and your family, really basic things like the way you look or practice your religion, or even your name," Mr. P said. Patty Zymont raised her hand.

"My great-grandfather had his name changed when he came to this country," Patty said. "He had a real long Czech name, and it was real hard to spell, and at immigration they said forget it, it's too long, and they just wrote down the first two syllables, Zymont."

"They cut off part of my great-grandfather's name, but I think it's because they didn't hear right," I said. "His name was Maslansky in Russia, but it came out Slansky on the forms, and that's been my mom's family name ever since."

"Both those examples are very typical of the Ellis

Island experience, which is the experience, I would guess, of at least half your great-grandparents," Mr. P said. "Names also got changed because immigrants mistook the question What's your name? for something else. My dad's family name was Leonetti in Italy, but when they asked my great-grandfather what his name was, he thought they were asking him where he was from, and he said, '*Sono padovano,*'—which means I'm a Paduan, I'm from Padua—and that became his name. A friend of mine has an unusual name because his grandfather confused What's your name? with What is your work? This happened to thousands of people, but this man had worked in a produce market, and when they translated what he said into English, his name became Fruithandler."

Everybody cracked up. Then I heard Jason Baron whisper to someone, "That should be Padovano's name," and I felt my mouth tighten angrily.

"What other changes can you think of that have taken place in your family since they arrived in America?" Mr. P asked.

"We're a lot less religious than my grandparents," Rachel Strauss said.

"Also a very common pattern," Mr. P said.

"Language," said Felicia Rim. "My grandparents never learned English, so my parents still speak Korean, but I only know a little."

"I have a great-grandma who's really tiny, like a first-grader, and my grandparents aren't much bigger," Eric Chang said. "My parents are about a foot taller than they are. My mom says it's because of better nutrition here."

20

"Excellent," Mr. P said. "Okay, now that we've got some ideas circulating, I'm gonna assign you a project." We all groaned except Holly. "I want you to dig up your family history, as far back as you can get information, focusing on your family's migration to this country. Show how your family's lives have changed because of the immigrant experience."

"I can't do that," Claudia van Zwolle wailed. "My family's lived around here since the 1600s!"

"Claudia, if your family's been here that long, they probably have a pretty good handle on their history and can tell you a lot, and I bet you can make use of the county historical society. You'll all be doing some book research for this paper, to get a general idea of the migration patterns of your ethnic group, or groups, as the case may be," Mr. P said. "But I want you to use primary sources as much as possible. That means letters, and documents like immigration forms, and it especially means talking to people, like your grandparents."

"I never see my grandparents," Jason Baron said. "I don't think I have too many relatives." A couple of other kids called out "Me neither."

"Well, now's a good time to find some," Mr. P said. "Talk to your parents tonight. They probably know more than you think they do. Talk to me if you get stuck. I'm going to want a list of definite and possible primary sources from all of you on Friday. Your project's due a month from today, but if you want to do a good job, you'll get started now."

When the bell rang, I asked Holly to wait until I gave back *A Tree Grows in Brooklyn* to Mr. P. She didn't seem to mind waiting; during class she'd passed me a note saying, "You're right, he's really cute."

"Did you like the book?" Mr. P asked.

"Oh, yeah," I said reverently. "When I finished, I wanted to go back and start reading it all over again."

"Good, I was hoping you'd like it," Mr. P said. "Holly, any questions you have about class or school so far?"

"No, I'm fine," she said. "This was the best class I had all day."

"Oh, well, then, you can definitely come back tomorrow," Mr. P said, which made Holly giggle. "Welcome to West River."

"See you tomorrow, Mr. P," I said.

As luck would have it, Kevin was just turning away from his locker across from Mr. P's room when we came out. My locker is between Mr. P's room and the one next door, and I usually try to hang out in Mr. P's room until Kevin heads for the bus. "It's no use, Huey," he said. "Tutti-Frutti can never be yours, unless you've got a sex organ none of us know about."

"Just ignore him," I said to Holly, who looked really mad.

"Still got your babe friend tagging along, I see," Kevin said, leering at Holly. "Want me to show you around? I'm a lot more fun than Baby Huey."

"Thanks, I'd rather sit in a mud puddle and have cockroaches crawl up my arm," Holly said.

"Wo, I'm crushed. How can I go on living?" Kevin came over and pretended to grab for my crotch. "You two make such a cute couple. Come on, you're hiding something in there, aren't you?" I jumped back. God, what a pig! "That's your secret, isn't it, Huey? Ooh, Tutti-Frutti's gonna be so happy when he finds out."

"Oh, you think anyone who isn't Rambo is gay," I said. I poked his chubby stomach. "Which makes me a little suspicious about *you*, lardo."

To my surprise, Kevin's face went white, and he charged me like an elephant, slamming me up against the lockers. "If I didn't just *think* you were a guy, I'd punch your lights out," he hissed. Then as fast as he rushed me, he moved back.

Mr. Padovano ran out of his room right after Kevin stepped away. He must have heard the thud when my back hit the lockers. By now about ten kids were watching. "What's going on?" Mr. P asked.

Holly was going to tell him, but I shook my head. "Nothing," I said. "We were having an argument."

"Are you all right?" Mr. P asked me. "Did he hit you?"

"N-no," I stammered, starting to move away from the lockers. "Everything's okay. I have to take Holly to the counselor and catch my bus."

"Okay, if you're sure," he said. "Break it up, every-body; go home."

Kevin marched off toward the buses, and the other kids turned back to their lockers or drifted away. "Thanks, Mr. P, I'm fine," I said. "Come on, Holly, we have to get to Ms. Hoxley quick; the buses are leaving soon."

Holly looked as if she wanted to talk about what happened at the lockers on our way to the counselor's office, but after a minute all she said was, "I'd invite you over, but we're still unpacking and our house is a mess. I probably won't have my room in shape until the weekend."

"That's okay, I have to go shopping with my mom this afternoon."

"Oh, that's fun."

"No, it's not," I said grimly. "Listen, you want my phone number? I should be home after seven."

"Sure, here's mine." We wrote down our numbers and traded.

The ten-after-three bell rang. "Oh, God, we'd better run, that bell means the buses are gonna leave," I said.

We both just made our buses. I wasn't looking forward to getting on the bus with Kevin on it, but he didn't say a word all the way home.

4

When I got home, I dropped my backpack on the chair in the front hall and went to the kitchen to get something to eat. My sister, Kim, was in the family room, giving half her attention to a math worksheet and half to Phil Donahue. "How can you watch that junk?" I asked through a mouthful of leftover spaghetti.

"It's interesting," she said, pointing at the TV. "All those people came back from the dead."

My mother's voice rose from the basement. "Jaaaaan?" she said.

"Yeah, Mom."

She came upstairs and into the family room, holding a basket of folded towels. "I wanna leave in five minutes."

"Okay, I just have to wash my face," I said.

"And make your bed. Why do I have to tell you every single day?"

"I was in a hurry this morning, okay? Did you want me to miss the bus?"

Mom gave me an I'm-not-buying-that look. "You're not in a hurry every morning, and every day I have to remind you or you don't do it."

"Okay, okay." I put the spaghetti back in the fridge and went through the family room toward the stairs.

Mom was taking another look at Kim. "Kimberly, what'd I tell you about doing your homework in front of the TV?"

Kim gave her a pleading look. "It's just math, Mom. It's simple."

"We've had this discussion before, Kim. No TV till your homework's done."

"You can't do that to her, Mom," I said from the stairs, fake-horrified. "If Kim doesn't get to watch her talk shows, she'll shrivel up and die."

"I'll take that chance," Mom said drily. "You hurry up and get ready or we won't have time to see Bubbie before we go home."

The only thing I hate worse than shopping for clothes is shopping for clothes with my mother. Okay, I should lose weight, and someday I will, but even if I did, I'd still have a weird body. Nothing ever fits; if it's okay on top or around the waist, it's tight in the belly and hips, and if it fits around the hips, there's about three extra inches around the waist and you could stuff pillows in the chest. My dad's built the same way, real pear-shaped.

My attitude toward clothes is: Okay, I'm a blimp, so throw a tent over me and leave me alone. Left to myself, I pick out clothes in dark colors with lots and lots of fabric. My goal is to be invisible from the neck down. That's usually what I wind up with, too, but not without a fight. Mom keeps wanting me to wear fashionable clothes, the kind they show in newspaper ads. I tell her I'd look ridiculous in them, she tells me not to be stubborn and try them on, I try them on and look ridiculous, and she tells me I could wear anything if I lost weight, which is B.S. if you ask me.

I don't know why, but Mom seems to take it personally that I don't look like her and don't care about clothes. I'm already a few inches taller than she is and of course much heavier. She has a pretty good figure. Even though she has a little potbelly, no one could call her fat, and she has a big chest that she's waiting for me to show signs of inheriting. (Nothing so far.) I just take after my father, that's all. I've got the same frizzy dark hair, except I'm not losing mine, same hazel eyes, same longish nose. It all looks better on him than me.

This shopping trip was like all the others. Mom dragged me into a junior department and went "ooh" and "aah" over how cute the new styles are, and I tried to squeeze into a couple of size-thirteens, and she finally settled for buying me a skirt from the fat-lady store. That's another reason I hate shopping; half the time I have to get stuff from stores that sell clothes in extralarge sizes. Anyway, Mom gave up on me sooner than she usually does and concentrated on Kim, who's a nice normal ten-year-old size and loves clothes.

We only went to one mall, Paramus Park, mostly because one of the department stores, A & S, was having a big sale. That's pretty restrained for my mother. Paramus is like a huge shopping mall—I don't think anyone actually lives there—and since Mom loves to shop more than anything else in the world, Paramus to her is like Mecca to a Muslim. But she had us in and out of there pretty fast so we could get to Bubbie.

Bubbie, my grandmother, owns a dress shop just outside one of New Jersey's ritziest malls. She opened it with the insurance money she got when my grandfather died, right after my mother graduated from college. By that time she'd been working in department stores for years and years and really knew the clothing business. So she opened this store, Sophisticated Lady, and it's been a big success from the start. It's mostly what Bubbie calls "special occasion" dresses for older women; she says she's dressed every mother of the bride in northern New Jersey for the past twenty years, and she probably isn't exaggerating much.

Bubbie is my all-around favorite, *favorite* person on earth. She's everything you want a grandmother to be: warm and huggy and generous, interested in everything Kim and I do, full of praise and good advice. And I admire her more than almost anybody else I know. I mean she is *really* smart, both in a business way and a personal way. Like a few years ago she noticed that a lot more women were working in executive jobs, so she started selling really pretty women's suits. All the mothers of the brides started sending their yuppie daughters to Bubbie for office clothes. Smart, huh? Plus she reads a lot; she belongs to some book club where they sit around and discuss books on important issues in society. And she's worked all her life, even when my mother and Uncle Steve were little. She's in her late sixties and still works a full day every day.

Sometimes I can't believe that Mom is her daughter. Mom's a college graduate, but she hardly reads anything except spy novels and murder mysteries. Bubbie knows twice as much as Mom does about current events, and she never went to college; her parents were poor and she had to work. Mom hasn't worked since before I was born; all she seems to do is shop, visit her friends (though not so much lately because most of *them* work now), and think of ways to redecorate our house. Well, she does do volunteer work, but I wouldn't call that a career. I think it's very interesting that Mom is all worried about how I look, and Bubbie, who's been selling clothes for more than forty years, keeps telling her that what's inside is more important and to quit nagging me. My life would be a lot easier if (1) Mom were more like Bubbie or (2) I were more like Mom. Personally, I'd pick (1).

Sherry, Bubbie's assistant, looked up from a clipboard she was writing on when she heard us come in. "Myra, your daughter is here," she called toward the back of the store. "Hi, Mrs. Green."

"Hi, Sherry," Mom said.

Bubbie came into the main part of the store, followed by a woman Mom's age or a little older who was wearing a long dark blue dress with a slash of silver from one shoulder to her hip. "Look, isn't she stunning?"

"That's very striking," Mom said.

"It's *too* striking," the woman said. "I don't want to take attention away from Nancy."

"What's wrong with looking beautiful?" Bubbie asked. "Instead of saying, 'What a beautiful bride,' they'll say, 'What a beautiful bride, just like her mother.'"

"But it's so dark, it's almost black," the woman said. "And the cut—"

"Don't worry, you have the neck for it. And dark is very stylish now for weddings. It's a Saturday night, it's winter." Bubbie lowered her voice as if she were telling a secret. "Let *his* mother look dowdy."

"You look glamorous," I said. "Like an actress going to the Oscars."

"Lillian, if you're not comfortable, I'll show you something else, but it really is stunning," Bubbie said.

"No, it's good," she said. I could tell from how she smiled into the mirror that she liked what she saw. "I'll take it." After Bubbie smiled her back into the try-on room, I put my hand up and she slapped me a high five.

"You are some saleswoman, Ma," Mom said. "That's no mother-of-the-bride dress."

"Shh!" Bubbie whispered. "The wedding's gonna be at the Pierre. She can wear whatever she wants."

Mom gave Bubbie some sheets and pillowcases she bought at A & S and started looking through the suits while Bubbie asked Kim and me about school. I told her about meeting Holly and how smart she is and how we seem to have a lot in common. "We probably won't wind up being friends, though."

"Why not?" Bubbie asked.

"Well, she's almost a year older than I am, and she's really pretty," I said. "She'll probably wind up making friends with the student-council kids."

"Don't be silly, darling," Bubbie said. "If she's as smart as you say, she'll want to be your friend because you're a wonderful person."

30

"That's not how kids make friends, Ma," my mother said. "It's as much the way you look as what kind of person you are. That's why I want you to wear nice clothes and fix your hair, darling," she said to me. "If you walk around looking schlumpy, people think you're a schlump."

"Okay, I'm a schlump," I said. "Face it, Mom, I'm never gonna be popular."

"Let her be, Carol," Bubbie said. "Isn't it enough that Janice has a good heart and a wonderful mind? Don't worry, she'll make friends."

"Can't someone be smart and popular at the same time?" Mom said.

"Not at my school," I said darkly.

Mom went to the store's restroom, and while she was gone I told Bubbie about the family history project for Mr. P. She said she'd sit down with me soon and tell me stories about her parents and grandparents, and she even promised to look for some old letters she said might still be around.

When Mom came back, she said it was time to go home and started to get Kim from where she was trying on hats. "Wait, Carol, I wanted to tell you something," Bubbie said. "You remember Sylvia Wyman, from Mayfair Drive?"

"Yeah," Mom said. "How is she?"

"She's fine, but remember her son Harold?" Mom nodded. "He and his wife just split up," Bubbie said.

"Really?" Mom said. "What happened?"

"He fell in love," Bubbie said. Mom shrugged, like that's nothing unusual, and Bubbie got this funny little smile on her face. "With *another man.*"

Mom's mouth fell open and I snorted. "You're kidding," Mom gasped.

"No, it's true," Bubbie said. "Sylvia told me he moved out last week."

"Did he move in with the other guy?" Mom asked in a horrified voice.

"No, he took an apartment in West Orange. Two bedrooms, for when his boys visit."

"My God, do they know?" Mom said.

"I think so," Bubbie said matter-of-factly.

"Is Sylvia upset? Did she know?"

"She told me she knew something was a little off with Harold, but she could never put her finger on it, and as soon as he told her, everything was clear."

"What about his wife?" Mom asked.

"Sylvia says she knew a long time already."

"Good Lord, Hal Wyman's gay," Mom said. "He used to play basketball with Stevie. I went out with him a couple of times in high school!"

"Don't worry, Mom, I don't think it's catching," I said.

Mom gave me a keep-out-of-this look. "Does he have AIDS?" she asked Bubbie.

"I don't think so," Bubbie said.

"Not everybody who's gay has AIDS, Mom," I said.

"I know that, Janice," Mom said.

Kim had come over and heard the end of the conversation. "Who's gay?" she asked.

"Nobody," Mom said.

"Some guy Mom used to date," I said.

"You went on a date with someone who's gay?" Kim asked.

Mom gave me a look that could melt diamonds, then turned back to Kim. "Kimberly, this is not something you need to know about."

"This guy Mom and Uncle Steve knew in high school just broke up with his wife because he's gay," I explained.

"Oh," Kim said. "Was he in denial?"

"What?" Mom said, startled.

"Sometimes gay people stay married for a long time because they have kids and they don't want to mess up their families," Kim said, "and sometimes they don't want to admit they're gay. That's called denial."

"How do you *know* this?" Mom asked.

"It was on 'Oprah,' " Kim said.

Daddy was waiting for us in the family room, already in flannel pajamas, when we got home a little after seven, loaded down with bags full of clothes and a ton of Chinese takeout. It was nice to see Daddy home so early. He's in business for himself and works superlong hours. When I was younger there were weeks I wouldn't see him from Monday to Friday.

I told my parents about the assignment to do a family history while we vacuumed up lemon chicken and fried rice. Daddy said it sounded interesting, but Mom didn't look happy. She's not too crazy about Mr. Padovano's special projects. For two weeks in September, he had us write down every time we heard someone say something prejudiced, whether it was racist, sexist, antigay, or against anybody's ethnic group, and I wrote down more stuff Mom said than anybody else except Kevin. Then last month we were studying environmental problems around the world, and we were all supposed to start recycling stuff at home. Mom said there was no way she was going to let her house become a garbage dump and start schlepping bottles and cans all over town, and I had to nag her for days until she let me collect aluminum cans.

Anyway, I got Daddy talking about his family, and he told me his grandfather had a brother who was an accountant for the Mafia in the 1920s and 1930s, which I thought was pretty interesting, since everybody in Daddy's family is an accountant going back around three generations, and accountants are supposed to be totally dull. Daddy used to be an accountant, but now he's in import-export, which means he buys and sells stuff from different countries. So Daddy's great-uncle helped hide a lot of mob money and then left for the Bahamas when the FBI started closing in. Mom about had a cow listening to Daddy, like it was some horrible family secret.

"This is so cool," I breathed. "I thought our family was totally boring, and we've got a gangster!"

"Are you happy now?" Mom asked Daddy. "She's thrilled that your grandfather's brother was a crook."

"Janice, Uncle Nate didn't run around with a machine gun," Daddy said. "He just kept the books."

"It's still the Mafia," I said. "He was like the God-father with a calculator!"

I was putting stuff in the dishwasher when the phone rang. Mom answered it and handed it to me.

It was Holly. "I just wanted to thank you for showing me around today, and for the notebook."

"Oh, no problem," I said, astonished that Holly had actually called me.

"Did that guy bother you on the bus?" she asked.

"No, he didn't say anything," I said, sitting at the kitchen table. Mom, who had been putting away the leftovers, gave me a dirty look and started putting the silverware in the dishwasher herself.

"I think you should tell the assistant principal, or at least Mr. Padovano."

"Really, Holly, it was no big deal. My shoulder hit the locker; it didn't even hurt."

"What happened, did somebody push you?" Mom asked.

"By accident, Mom. Wait a sec, Holly." I put my hand over the receiver. "This guy tripped in the hall after school and accidentally pushed me against the lockers. I'm fine," I told Mom.

"Is that the girl you were telling us about?" Mom asked.

"Yeah," I said. Mom made a face like oh-how-nice and went into the family room. "Hi, I'm back," I said to Holly.

"How was shopping?" she asked.

"Horrible, as usual. I wish she'd just give up. No matter what I try on, I look like a freak."

"Maybe we can go shopping this weekend. My mom can probably take us."

"Sure," I said, thrilled to death. Somehow shopping with Holly sounded like a lot more fun than shopping with Mom. "Did you tell your parents about the family history?"

"Yeah," Holly said. "They think it's really interest-

35

ing. My dad has some stuff his great-grandparents brought from Norway, and he said I could show it in class."

"I found out something *so cool*," I said, unfortunately just as Mom came back in and opened the freezer. "My father told me his grandfather's brother worked for the Mafia!"

"JANICE!" Mom screamed.

"Wow," Holly said admiringly.

❧ 5 ❧

A few weeks after Holly and I met, we were sitting in Mr. Padovano's room after school with twenty other kids, trying out for the Academic All-Stars, a team that competes with other junior highs in a contest every March. One of the qualifying tests was an essay based on a quotation from Mark Twain, and as soon as I read "Few things are harder to put up with than the annoyance of a good example," I knew exactly what to write about.

My mother calls my younger sister her little ray of sunshine, and sometimes I think that makes me her dark cloud. It's not that my sister's a phony or a suck-up—she's just naturally sunny—but when Mom gets going about how helpful and cheerful and sweet she is, it's Kim that I want to rain on.

We all scribbled away like maniacs except Holly, who does all her work slowly and steadily—and perfectly, like she does everything else.

The other golden girls had tried to make friends with Holly—Heather Rubin had even invited her to a party—but Holly had told Heather she was busy, and she kept hanging out with us nerdettes like a bluebird in a nest of sparrows. She and I were best friends. I couldn't believe it, but we were. She told me how she wanted to be an architect and figure out ways to build beautiful apartments cheaply so no one would be homeless anymore, and she told me how last year this friend of her father's got drunk and put his hand on her behind and she told her mom and her mom almost killed the guy, and all kinds of other personal stuff.

She said it really wasn't that great being pretty, which is also kind of hard to believe. "When people meet me, they assume I'm an airhead because I look like what they *think* pretty is," she said one day. "Then when I show some brains, they act all offended, like I'm not supposed to be smart too. I hate the way you're supposed to be one or the other. That's why I can't stand Heather and that student-council crowd, because a lot of them really are smart but they act like they wish they weren't, and they only use their brains to play their stupid little social games."

Before Holly moved to West River, I'd hung around with kids in our neighborhood and been to my share of parties, but Holly was the first kid I'd ever met who seemed to care enough to sort of root for me. We went to the mall, and she showed me stuff to wear that made me look thinner and was almost cool. She admired my articles in the school newspaper and lent me books to read. Somehow she was able to freeze loudmouths like Kevin Lynch with a single look, to where Kevin actually quit bothering me when Holly was around. If she'd ridden my bus to school, my life would have been perfect.

So there we were trying out for the All-Stars, the one big-deal school activity that makes temporary heroes out of nerds at West River Junior High. The team is supposed to have three groups of three kids each, A-average, B-average, and C-average—only they call it Honors, Scholastic, and Varsity—so it isn't just Nerd City. Besides the essay, we had to take quizzes in math, science, and history. Holly and I thought we had a good chance because Mr. P, the head coach, had more or less recruited us. "I'd like to see Sheila, Rachel, and Felicia try out too," he told us.

"You'll never get Felicia," I said. "She hangs out with Heather, so the All-Stars aren't cool enough for her. But we'll work on the others." As it turned out, Rachel was already planning to try out, and she was sitting in front of me, looking around nervously from time to time as if she thought somebody was copying her essay. We got Sheila to come too, though that was harder, because she's incredibly shy and hates doing anything in a group. She was in a back corner, all elbows and neck (she's even taller than I am), alternately biting her pen and writing in what I knew was her tiny, tiny printing. I concentrated on writing the best essay I could before the late bus left.

Mr. P didn't leave us hanging long. Holly and I got invitations to join the team in homeroom two days later, and at lunch we found out that Sheila did too, but Rachel didn't. She was pretty bummed out about it.

"It was really stiff competition," I said. "It doesn't mean you're not smart."

"It means I'm not as smart as you guys," Rachel said.

"That's silly," Holly said. "You're just as smart as we are. You were just having a bad day or something."

"But I really wanted to make the team," Rachel said. "I mean, what's the good of being a nerd if you can't make the All-Stars?"

"You mean what's good about being smart? Plenty," Holly said.

"Yeah," I said, gesturing around the room with a fork full of pasta salad. "For starters, you'll be finding a cure for cancer while half of these doofy girls will be spraying cologne on people in department stores."

"That doesn't do me any good now," Rachel said. "I feel kind of left out."

"We're not gonna quit talking to you, Rache," I said. "Come on, we're the Read-a-Book-a-Week-at-Lunch Bunch."

"You can't get rid of us that easy," Holly said. "Besides, in a few weeks we'll be complaining about how hard we're working, and you'll be thinking we were crazy to go out for the team in the first place!" That made Rachel look a little less sad.

"If it means that much to you, you can have my place on the team," Sheila said. I gave her a look like *Are you nuts?*

Rachel thought about it for a second, then shook her head. "No, if Mr. P picked you, it's 'cause you're better for the team. Maybe I'll start taking guitar lessons. My mom's after me to pick a new instrument since I quit piano."

Mr. P asked Holly, Sheila, and me to stay after class that day. Rachel sort of hung out in the doorway until Mr. P told her that she really had done very well and it had been tough to make a decision. "I may just turn to you if I have a dropout before January," he said. That made Rachel look even less sad, and she went home. Then Sheila started again with how Rachel could have her place. I swear, she is so modest. I think if Sheila ever wins the Nobel Prize, which she probably will, she'll just say thank you and ask them to give it to whoever came in second.

"That's isn't how it works, kiddo—you're the one I want," Mr. P said. "Holly's superstrong in math, and Janice wrote the best essay, but, Sheila, you were just all-round fabulous." Sheila blushed. She's been one of the smartest kids in school since kindergarten, but I don't think she's used to being told she's fabulous. He smiled at Sheila, really turning on the charm. "You wouldn't let me down, would you, Sheila?" He made a funny, pleading face. "Come on, Sheila, we need you. Pleeeeease?" Sheila finally giggled and said okay. "Oh, thank goodness," Mr. P said with exaggerated relief. "I'll be able to sleep tonight."

"Who else is on the team?" Holly asked.

"Um, for Scholastic level, Shawn Choi and Ron Kempner," Mr. P said. We all nodded; they're ninth-graders we've had classes with. "And an eighth-grader, Cory Grainger—very sharp kid."

"What about Varsity?" Holly asked.

"Actually, I need to talk to Janice about that," Mr. P said. "I'm having a little trouble."

The bus bell rang. "I can't stay, Mr. P," I said. "The bus is gonna leave."

"How about a ride then?" Mr. P said. "I might as well find out where you all live. I'll be taking you home lots of afternoons once practice starts."

We all got into Mr. P's car, a gray Nissan. He took Sheila home first because she lives near school and then headed toward the side of West River where Holly and I live. "What did you want to talk to me about?" I asked.

"You can wait till you drop me off if you want," Holly said.

"Oh, it's no big secret," Mr. P said. He glanced at me. "Janice, what would you think of having Kevin Lynch on the All-Stars?"

"Ugh," Holly said disgustedly from the backseat. I bent forward and pretended to throw up on the floor of the car: *Bleaaaaaggggh!*

Mr. P looked amused. "Are you voicing opposition?"

I turned around to Holly, and we gave each other a horrified look. "Mr. P, you have got to be kidding," I said.

"I'm absolutely stuck for Varsity students," Mr. P said. "And I think Kevin is the kind of kid we need."

"Does he even have a C average?" I asked. "I think he mostly does his homework on the bus, when he does it at all."

Mr. P nodded. "He's eligible."

"But why would you want *Kevin?*" Holly asked. "There are probably lots of kids with C averages who are nicer and work harder."

"To put it bluntly, they're usually not as smart," Mr. P said. "I need the kids who get lower grades because they're lazy or they think school is stupid. And

42

of course most of those kids won't go out for the All-Stars—it's too much work and it means you're a nerd. I found that out last year."

"Is Kevin really that smart?" Holly asked.

"In a word, yes," Mr. P said. "He was in one of my U.S. history classes for a while last year, and—well, trust me, he is."

We got to Holly's house, and Holly thanked Mr. P and jumped out. "Janice, if you really think Kevin wouldn't be suitable for the All-Stars, I won't try to recruit him, but I really am desperate for Varsity kids," Mr. P said.

"Well, I guess he is sort of smart," I said, remembering the hard time he gave our teacher back in sixth grade. He used to drive Ms. Farrell crazy asking questions. Like when we were studying the Constitution, he'd ask her all about these Supreme Court decisions, and he'd know more about them than she did. After a while she'd tell him to be quiet, and he'd say, "What's the matter, Ms. Farrell, don'tcha read the newspaper?" Then she'd send him to the principal's office. I've also seen him reading interesting stuff on the bus, like *Rolling Stone* magazine. "But Mr. P, he's so awful!"

Mr. P stopped at a red light and smiled at me. "Sometimes when a kid gets involved in something like this, he gets to be less awful."

"But he won't do it," I said. "I'll bet you a million dollars."

"Maybe, but I figure it's worth a try," Mr. P said. "I was hoping you could soften him up for me."

"What?" I said incredulously. "Mr. P, Kevin Lynch hates my guts! You know he does! He's ragged on me since elementary school! He slammed me into the lockers!"

Mr. P nodded thoughtfully. "Yeah, I remember that."

"I don't know why, but he hates me, and he always has," I said sullenly. "I'm the last person who should talk to him about anything."

"Well, this may not make much sense, but just because someone insults you, that doesn't mean he doesn't respect you."

"Yeah, right, Kevin's always showing how much he respects me," I said sarcastically. I really wanted to talk Mr. P out of this. "You know, he doesn't like you either, Mr. P. He says mean things about you too." Please don't ask me what, I begged silently.

"I can imagine," Mr. P said. "Still, Janice, even if there's a one-in-a-hundred chance he'll be on the team, we ought to go for it. And I bet approaching Kevin about the team will make you less scared of him."

"I'm not scared of Kevin Lynch," I said, majorly insulted.

"Okay," he said. "Then just do it for the team, huh?"

"Oh, all right, but it won't work," I said as the car pulled up in front of my house. When you get right down to it, short of selling drugs, there isn't anything I wouldn't do for Mr. Padovano.

6

Mom was pleased when I told her I'd made it onto the Academic All-Stars, though a little excitement would have been nice. Later I heard her telling a friend on the phone, so I guess she was pretty happy about it.

The next morning I took my time getting to the bus stop and had to run past the last couple of houses to make it onto the bus. Kevin saw me pant up the steps and called out, "And bringing up the rear, and I do mean rear, number seven, Baby Huey!"

I flopped into my usual seat. Forget it, Mr. P, you're on your own. But I remembered the stuff he'd said in the car about respect and Kevin's being smart and needing him for the team, and as the bus picked up the last kids and headed down Shoemaker Road toward the middle of town, I went back to where Kevin was sitting. "Can I talk to you for a second?" I asked.

"Sure, Huey," Kevin said, motioning to the seat in front of him. "Step into my office."

"Not here," I said, gesturing to seats a few rows

away. "Up there." The idiots who sit behind Kevin went "Ooooooooooh," as if I were flirting with him or something. I rolled my eyes and gave them a drop-dead-you-morons look, and I saw Kevin half turn around and do the same. He didn't look like he wanted to move, so I said, "Please, it's important."

To my surprise, Kevin got up, and we moved up about four rows, Kevin sitting behind me. "What's so important?" he asked.

"You know the Academic All-Stars?" I asked.

"Yeah," he said.

"Mr. Padovano asked me to ask you if you'd go out for the team."

"Are you kidding?" Kevin said, not looking very pleased.

"No, he asked me to ask you," I said. "He doesn't have enough team members with your grade point average."

"What does he want *me* for?" he asked.

"I don't know," I said. "He seems to think you're smarter than you act." I tried to sound as if I didn't really believe it but he should go out for the team anyway.

"Is that right?" Kevin said sarcastically. "Did he say *why* I should enter the Valley of the Nerds?"

"What do you mean?"

"I mean what's in it for me? I've got better things to do with my time."

"I don't know what's in it for you," I said impatiently. "I know someone who was on the team last year. She said it took a lot of time and you had to work hard, but it was worth it because you learned a lot and the school makes a fuss over you. The assembly on competition day is pretty cool—you march in and everybody gets a trophy."

"Wow, a trophy," Kevin said, even more sarcastically. "I don't think so, Huey. Tell Tutti-Frutti if he's hot for my tender young body, he can say it with flowers."

"You're totally disgusting, you know that?" I said. "Sorry I said anything." I jumped up and practically ran back to my usual seat.

On my way to math, I stopped by Mr. P's room. "I asked Kevin, Mr. P, but he's not interested, believe me."

"Okay, Janice, I thought it was worth a shot. Thanks a lot." Yeah, thanks a lot, Mr. P, I thought, choking back an I-told-you-so.

I thought that was the end of it, but during lunch I saw Mr. P come into the cafeteria and stand by the door, scanning the room a couple of times but mostly watching Kevin, who wandered around the room with his tray for a few minutes and finally sat down by himself, took a comic book out of his back pocket, and read while he ate. I got interested and started watching Mr. P watch Kevin. "What are you looking at?" Holly asked.

"I don't think Mr. P's given up on Kevin for the team," I said. "He's standing over there scoping him out."

"Maybe Mr. P likes him," Rachel said. She and Holly giggled.

"Oh, Rachel, not you too," I said.

"Besides, even if Mr. P *is* gay, he can do a lot better than Kevin," Holly said. She and Rachel laughed harder. Sheila, who was reading *Pudd'nhead Wilson*, the book we had to read for the All-Stars, turned bright red. Mr. P looked as if he was going to try to see what Kevin was reading, then thought better of it and left.

In period six, Mr. P checked the first drafts of our family histories and sprang the what-if part of the project on us: Write an essay of at least a page describing what you think your life would be like now if your great-grandparents or other ancestors had not left their native lands and come to this country. Everybody looked confused and started talking at once. "Use your knowledge of current conditions in those countries to support your descriptions," Mr. P said.

A lot of the Jewish kids looked a little spooked, realizing that if their ancestors hadn't left Europe, they might have gotten killed in the Holocaust, but not Jason Baron, who isn't exactly Mr. Sensitivity. "Hey, I'll be able to write this essay in about two seconds," he said. "All my grandparents would have been killed by the Nazis, and I wouldn't have been born." Holly and I exchanged a what-a-bozo look.

"At least a page, Jason," Mr. P said. "Use a little imagination. I understand this idea might be painful for some of you kids, but I'm not trying to make the essay an exercise in victimization. Let's assume that *someone* survived to produce you."

Just before the end of the period, Kevin came in holding a summons, and Mr. P wrapped up his instructions. "You're dismissed when the bell rings," he said. "Don't forget, quiz tomorrow."

I did my best to listen in on their conversation, though it wasn't easy with Heather Rubin and Patty

Zymont babbling away in front of me. Mr. P thanked Kevin for coming in, and Kevin said, "I know what you want to see me about, but I'm not interested." Then the bell rang, and everybody picked up their stuff and headed out. I closed my notebook s-l-o-o-o-w-l-y. Motioning with my head to Holly, I went to the back of the room to look at some dioramas Mr. P's period-four class had made.

"... I also think you might find this class more challenging than your present world geography," Mr. P was saying.

"Listen, Mr. Padovano, I'm flattered and all, but my program's okay the way it is, and the All-Stars team isn't my kind of scene," Kevin said.

"A little too nerdy?" Mr. P said.

Kevin gave him a hint of a smile. "Yeah, you might say that."

"Afraid your friends might give you a hard time?" It seemed like Mr. P came down a little hard on the word *friends*.

For some reason, Kevin looked uncomfortable. "I don't worry about what other people think," he said after a moment. "I'm just not interested, that's all."

Mr. P sighed, but almost in a fake way. "Well, I'm sorry to hear that, Kevin, because I think you'd be a tremendous asset to the team."

"Tremendous is right," I muttered to Holly.

Mr. P looked over at us. "Janice, Holly, do you need me for something?" We said no. "Then would you excuse us, please?"

We started out, taking our time, while Kevin said, "I've gotta catch my bus, Mr. Padovano."

"I'll let you go in just a second," he said, giving us a real get-out-of-here look. Holly went off to her locker, but I hung out across the hall and watched them through Mr. P's open door, or actually watched Kevin's back, which completely blotted out Mr. P. Then I got out of the way fast, because Kevin came striding out of Mr. P's room, looking totally P.O.'d, and slammed his locker open like he couldn't wait to get out of the building.

On the bus home he read his comic book again, but as I was getting off, he said, "Hey, Green."

"What?" I said. He knew if he called me Huey I wouldn't answer.

"Keep your fat ass out of my business and your homo friend Padovano away from me." I marched off the bus, wondering what Mr. P had said to get Kevin so angry.

The next day was Friday, and my mother was picking me up early for a dental appointment, so I left Mr. P's class right after the quiz to cut through the teachers' parking lot and meet Mom at the school's side gate. As I came out the side door, I saw a tall, hulking figure, parka hood pulled up, rise from the middle of the teachers' cars, a spray paint can in his hand. I'd know that parka anywhere.

Kevin didn't see me as he admired his artwork, the word *FAGGOT* sprayed in lavender across the driver's side doors of Mr. P's gray Nissan. I couldn't believe anyone who was supposed to be smart was dumb enough not to stay down and jam out of there immediately. When I got about two cars away from him, I smiled nastily and said, "Nice work, Picasso."

50

He spun around, still clutching the spray can, and stared at me in horror. Then he came out from between the cars and ran out the gate and across the street, disappearing between two houses.

My thrill at catching Kevin doing something totally criminal quickly faded as I thought of all the people who might see that word before Mr. P got to his car. I couldn't report Kevin to the assistant principal without them knowing what was written on the car. Maybe Mr. P had a cover for the car, and if I went back and told him his car had been vandalized, he could cover it fast and stay at school until everyone had left. Even if he didn't have a cover, at least he'd know what had happened before everybody else did. But just as I turned to go back into school, my mother pulled up along the fence and honked.

Mom hates to be kept waiting more than anything else in the world, and if I went back into the building now, she'd be mad at me for weeks. She rolled down the window of her tank-sized station wagon and yelled, "Let's go, Janice, we're late!"

I hesitated for a moment. I couldn't tell her about Mr. P's car; she wouldn't understand. "I have to go back in, Mom," I said through the fence. "I forgot something."

"Well, you can get it from Holly or it can wait till Monday," Mom said angrily. "I'm not going to keep Dr. Weisman waiting just because you forgot something. It was hard enough to get this appointment."

"Mom, it's important," I pleaded.

"If it was that important, you would have remembered," she said. "Let's go, right now!"

That was that. If I went into school, she'd probably

51

come after me. Mom pulled up to the gate and I got in the car. As soon as I closed the door, she tore down the street like it was the Indianapolis 500, which is how she always drives. Daddy's always telling her one day she's gonna hit somebody. I just hoped today was the day and the person she ran over was Kevin.

Dr. Weisman drilled and filled two cavities. As punishment for not warning Mr. P, it was a start, I decided, but not enough.

❧ 7 ❧

The next day was Saturday. I still had a terrible case of the guilts, thinking about all the kids and teachers who must have seen Mr. P's car Friday after school. More than anything, I wanted to do something for Mr. P, and over my Wheat Chex I had an idea.

There were a lot of Lynches in the Orchard County phone book, but only one in West River in the development just the other side of Shoemaker Road from ours, which is where our school bus route starts. I got Kevin on the phone and told him I was coming over and he'd better be there if he knew what was good for him. He didn't even protest.

Around ten-thirty I told Mom I was walking over to Holly's house. "You want me to drive you? I'm going food shopping downtown in a little while," she said.

"No, thanks," I said. "I want to get some exercise."

"Okay, sweetheart," she said. *Exercise* is a magic word for her. She never does any, but she's always nagging me about it.

I walked past the wood shingle and red brick houses in our development and crossed Shoemaker Road, which is like the dividing line between the old part of West River and the new part. Of course the old part isn't very old, since West River was just a tiny cluster of houses and shops around the courthouse downtown until the Thruway went through Orchard County in the 1950s. Then they knocked down all the apple and pear trees and built acres and acres of split-level houses that all look alike. Some of my friends live in them.

Where we live, the houses are newer and bigger, built on land that used to be woods. Then when they ran out of room to build houses, they started putting condos and apartments close to downtown, the kind of thing I guess Holly's dad is building.

It took me about fifteen minutes to walk to Kevin's house. His mom let me in and was very friendly when I introduced myself. Then Kevin loomed up behind her. "We can talk in my room," he said sourly.

Mrs. Lynch's face got a little worried. "Kevin, dear, I'm not sure that's appropriate," she said.

Kevin gave her a total give-me-a-break look. "She just needs to talk to me about something," he said disgustedly.

His room was downstairs and looked like a cave. He had the walls painted black, with some heavy-metal posters and others of musicians who looked like they were from the sixties, some of whom I recognized, like the Doors, and Jimi Hendrix, and Peter Townshend when he was young. He had some posters and photos of sports cars on the walls too. There was a huge boom box with radio, cassette deck, and CD player; an unmade bed; used plates and glasses all over; and books and magazines in huge piles on a beat-up desk and the floor. The room was lit by a lamp on the desk, and there was another lamp on an orange crate next to the bed.

Actually I thought his room was sort of cool, though a little dark. It couldn't have been more different from my bedroom, which is big and airy and reasonably neat when I make my bed. Mom won't let me put a lot of stuff on the walls—just a couple of framed art posters—and she makes me keep the clutter to one pile of magazines and papers on my desk. All the furniture is matching fake Early American. The only thing my room had in common with Kevin's was lots of books, but mine are all on bookshelves. Kevin's room was too small to have many bookshelves.

Kevin sat on the bed and offered me the desk chair. "Whatta you want?" he said.

I wanted to stretch out the moment a little. "You sure surprised me yesterday," I said.

"I surprised *you?*" he asked.

"Yeah," I said. "I didn't know a tub like you could run so fast."

Kevin's beady eyes narrowed as I started to laugh. "Awright, Huey, you've had your joke. Why are you here?" he demanded.

I stopped laughing. This was where I was going to get tough. "You're in a lot of trouble if I tell the school or the cops what you did."

Kevin tried to play it cool. "So?"

"So you could get suspended or even expelled."

"Big deal," he said. "So Christmas vacation starts early."

"They could arrest you. You could go to juvie."

"They're not gonna arrest a fourteen-year-old kid for a little spray-painting," Kevin said. "They'd probably just make me apologize and have my dad pay to have Padovano's car painted."

"How do you know?" I said. "You vandalized Mr. P's car and attacked him for being gay. That's a, what do you call it, a hate crime. They could throw you in juvie as an example, and Mr. P could sue you for libel."

"You mean slander," Kevin said. "Libel's in print, and in either case they have to prove what you said wasn't true."

"How do you know that?" I asked.

"I read it in the newspaper."

"Well, how do you know Mr. P is gay?"

"Jeez, you really are naive," he said. "Come on, Huey, Padovano's the biggest queer in a ten-mile radius."

"Okay, then he could sue you for, uh, violating his civil rights," I said. "I read the paper too, butthead."

"Oh, wake up," Kevin said impatiently. "Kids don't get sued for that. They think we're too stupid and we just get ideas like that from our folks. In fact, I could probably get out of the whole thing by playing dumb."

"In which case the lawyer would bring in your school records and show the judge that you're not, that you're actually very smart and knew exactly what you were doing," I said triumphantly. "And I could testify that you've been saying nasty things about Mr. P being gay all semester."

"Yeah, well, pigs do squeal," Kevin sneered.

"I'd rather be a squealer than see you get away with trashing Mr. P's car in front of the whole school," I said. "Say whatever you want, you committed a crime, and if I tell, you'll get in major trouble."

"Yeah, well, I don't think so," Kevin said, but he didn't sound as sure.

"Fine, maybe you're right," I said, getting up. "We'll find out after I call the cops. Bye." I started out.

"Wait a minute," Kevin said, standing up too. "You said I'd be in trouble *if* you told what I did. Does that mean maybe you won't?"

"What do you care?" I asked. "You don't think you'll get in trouble, so why worry about what I do? See ya." I was almost at the door of his room.

"Hold it," he said, and now he sounded a little panicky. "What do I have to do for you not to tell?"

"Sit down," I said, and he sat back on the bed. "I've got three conditions. First, you go out for the All-Stars, and I mean really do it, show up for all the practices, study whatever we have to study, no dissing the other team members, and don't like deliberately fail something so you're off the team. I think Mr. P's crazy to want you on the team, but at least this way you can partly make up to him for what you did."

"Yeah, okay," Kevin said. "What else?"

"You don't give Mr. P a hard time," I said. "If he wants you in our period six, you switch. And you act polite to him."

"Oh, come on, Huey, I give all the teachers a hard time."

"Not Mr. Padovano, not if you don't want a visit from the cops. I can't stop you from talking behind his back, but when he's around, you're gonna be Saint Kevin."

57

"All right, but the first time he comes on to me, all bets are off." I gave him an oh-please look. "What's the third condition?" he asked.

"You quit calling me Baby Huey, or Huey, or anything like it, and I mean forever," I said, pointing at him. "I can take all the fat jokes you can dish out. You wanna rag on me for being a nerd or pear-shaped or younger than everybody else, go ahead—you're not telling me anything I don't know. But you've called me Baby Huey for the last time."

"Get your finger out of my face," Kevin said. I put my finger down. "You're taking all the fun out of my life."

"If calling someone who never did anything bad to you the same stupid name for three solid years is your idea of fun, then I feel sorry for you," I said. "Anyway, those are my terms: Take 'em or leave 'em."

"Let me get this straight," he said. "I go out for the Nerd-Stars, I make nice with Tutti-Frutti, and the H word never passes my lips again, and in return no one finds out I decorated Padovano's car?"

"No one finds out from me," I said. "You have my word on it."

Kevin gave me a hard look, like he was trying to decide if he could trust me. "Okay," he finally said.

"Good," I said. I had the feeling Kevin would live up to his part of the deal, not so much because he was scared I'd squeal on him, but because he said he would. I don't know why I felt that way. I just did.

By Monday morning it was all over school that someone had spray-painted *FAGGOT* on Mr. P's car. In fact, it seemed to be everybody's hot topic all weekend. I first "heard" about it Saturday afternoon from Sheila, who heard it from Rachel, who heard it from this kid in our preconfirmation class who actually goes to Friday night services every week, and *she* heard it from the rabbi's son, who cuts through the faculty parking lot to walk home. I called Holly, but she had already heard it from somebody she ran into at the public library.

At school, most of the girls either were really mad that someone would do something that awful to Mr. P or didn't care, and most of the boys either thought it was really funny or didn't care. The teachers wouldn't deal with it at all. First thing Monday, Patty Zymont asked Ms. Zaiman if she'd heard about what happened to Mr. P's car, and she said, "Yes, and that closes the subject in this class. Open your books to page one hundred forty." And when Jason Baron asked Mr. Geiger if he spelled *faggot* with one *g* or two, Mr. Geiger said, "I don't spell it at all, and you just earned an hour's detention."

The worst moment I had all day was at lunch. By the time the bell was about to ring for activities, I was sick of hearing about Mr. P's car, and is-he-or-isn't-he-gay, and how-can-he-be-gay-he's-so-cute, and don't-be-stupid-all-gay-men-are-cute, and he-better-not-try-anything-funny-with-me, and oh-please-a-dog-wouldn't-touch-you, and you-would-know-huh. I was eating chocolate pudding and wishing the whole thing would go away when Holly asked, "Didn't you go past the teachers' cars Friday to meet your mom?"

"Uh, yeah," I said, hoping my face wasn't bright red.

"Was the writing already there when you went out?"

"Uh, I didn't see it," I lied, wishing she'd change the subject.

"Did you see anybody hanging around?"

"No," I said, trying to sound annoyed. "What are you, a cop?"

"Okay, sorry I asked," Holly said, sounding offended.

"Just quit talking about it, okay?"

Holly must have thought I didn't want to talk about it because I was hurting for Mr. P, because she stopped looking mad and said, "Okay, I'm sorry."

After lunch I went to work on the school newspaper. A couple of kids asked Ms. Perkins, the faculty adviser, if the newspaper should print anything about Mr. P's car, and she said probably not, because it would call attention to the incident and give the vandal attention he or she didn't deserve, plus it wouldn't make things any more pleasant for Mr. Padovano. Scott Confino, the news editor, argued that it was news, and Ms. Perkins said if every stupid prank kids played at West River Junior High was news, there wouldn't be room for anything else in the paper. So Liz Feinberg, who's editor-in-chief, asked if we could print an editorial about vandalism and hate language without naming any names, and Ms. Perkins said she'd talk to Mr. P and find out how he felt about it. On my way to English class I saw Kevin, who hadn't been around at lunch, go up to Mr. P and talk to him.

Period six was really weird. All the boys who'd been making rude comments about Mr. P all day shut up, and all the girls stared at him pityingly like he had some kind of terminal disease and didn't know it. We were studying Japan, and Mr. P was trying to get us to

60

discuss what's in the textbook about Japan compared to what we hear about Japan in the media, but nobody had anything to say. Finally he gave up and assigned us an essay for homework and said we could start now.

He didn't say anything about his car, but just before the period was over he said, "Oh, Holly, Janice, Sheila, I finally filled out the Varsity team, so we'll have our first meeting tomorrow." He looked at me and said, "Janice, you owe me a million dollars."

8

Life got so full of stuff to do that I practically had to quit watching TV. Let me tell you, "Roseanne" is a lot funnier when it's the only thing you get to watch all evening.

I finished my family history project. For the what-if part I imagined Bubbie as this heroic teenaged Resistance fighter in the Warsaw ghetto who somehow escaped from the Nazis at the last minute and hid in a cave and came to America after the war. Then I volunteered for the first day of oral reports just to get mine out of the way. The class thought it was pretty cool that my dad's great-uncle had been an accountant for the Mob. So my report went okay, but Todd Ginsburg's was a lot more interesting because half his background is African. He said if his ancestors hadn't been brought to this country as slaves, he might be a Senegalese prince, because supposedly his mother was descended from a royal family there. Some of the kids started calling Todd Your Highness after that, but most of us thought being a prince was fairly impressive.

Practice for the All-Stars got started, three afternoons a week. The eighth-grader on the Scholastic
part of the team, Cory Grainger, was very quiet and
intense—and very smart. The other kid on the Varsity
team besides Kevin was another eighth-grader, Karen
Levant, who was very good at memorizing stuff. She
didn't seem like someone who'd have less than a B
average, but later she told us that her parents had bro-
ken up over the summer and her schoolwork had
seemed a little irrelevant during the fall, so her mid-
term report card was lousy. I don't know how Mr. P
found her, but she seemed like an excellent person to
have on the team.

Kevin showed up for every practice, just as he'd
promised. He'd sit apart from the rest of the team and
wouldn't say much unless Mr. P or the math and science coach, Mr. Perlman, asked him a direct question.
He was behind the rest of us in math, and Mr. P was
always trying to get him to write in more detail on the
practice essays, but he did well on all the social studies
quizzes we did as practice, and it turned out he had
already read *Pudd'nhead Wilson* and knew who all the
characters were and understood the whole book. It's a
pretty interesting story by Mark Twain about a slave in
Missouri who looks white and switches her baby with a
look-alike white baby so her child will grow up rich
and privileged. Her real son, called Tom, grows up and
turns out to be a real creep, but this lawyer in their
town, Pudd'nhead Wilson, figures out that the babies
were switched, and Tom gets sold as a slave at the end.

Kevin was way ahead of us with the book, which was
written about a hundred years ago and is pretty hard to
read. Mr. P was always complimenting him for his

insight into the book's characters and theme and historical background on the rare occasions Kevin bothered to answer a question. I wouldn't say Kevin was an enthusiastic teammate, but he didn't give Mr. P a hard time.

So December was incredibly busy, what with school and homework and All-Stars practice and preconfirmation class and shopping for holiday presents. I got Holly a huge T-shirt for sleeping in and she got me a great pair of earrings. Usually during Christmas vacation, I sleep till noon and just watch TV all day, but not this year, because I had all this studying and reading to do for the All-Stars. I almost forgot my birthday was coming until it did and I turned fourteen (finally).

The whispers about Mr. P's being gay died down during December, and I was hoping that with vacation coming, the holiday play, the start of the basketball season, and all the other December stuff, everybody would just forget the whole thing. But in January it all started up again.

Girls started passing around notes: "You think Padovano has a boyfriend?" "What do gay guys do together?" "What makes people gay?" Disgusting comments, some of them illustrated, began to appear on desks. Almost every day I had to wet a tissue and wipe out the charming remarks of some clown who had my desk in Mr. Geiger's classroom earlier in the day. It was the big topic of conversation at Holly's birthday party, which was a Sunday luncheon, very elegant and all girls, thank goodness. A lot of girls think that by the time you're fifteen you just have to have a party at night with boys, but I think Holly's idea was a lot more fun.

I came home the afternoon of parents' night to hear Mom on the phone with Bubbie. "For the eightieth time this week, Ma, stop nagging me to get a job! I have a perfectly fulfilling life without standing behind a counter or sitting at a desk all day! ... I don't care if I would have been a buyer by now.... I know this sounds weird to you, Ma, but I'd rather be at home for my kids.... I know you worked to give us things we wouldn't have had otherwise.... Of course I'm grateful, but I don't have to do what you did because Marty makes plenty of money.... The card game was only once a week, Ma, I don't miss it.... I don't care if the girls are big now, my job is raising them and keeping a nice house, and I don't want to work anywhere else!"

I hung up my coat and took my backpack upstairs. I'm with Bubbie; I wish Mom would get a job. Everybody I know, their mothers work, even the rich ones. Like Holly's—her dad makes lots of money, but Mrs. Johansen says she'd go nuts if she had to hang around West River with nothing to do all day. I also happen to know that Mom does miss her card game. She used to play bridge in New Jersey every Tuesday with these women she grew up with, but one by one they all went to work and couldn't play anymore. Mom and this one other lady couldn't find replacements, and finally they just had to quit last year.

It was nice when I was little. I'd come home from school, and Mom would have cookies and milk waiting and want to hear all about my day. I'd tell her, while Kim and her little friends played with blocks or dolls on the kitchen floor. Now when I come home, Kim's in front of the TV putting off doing her homework, and

Mom doesn't let me eat cookies because I'm too fat, and I don't want to tell her anything that happened at school. If I get a ninety-eight on a test, she wants to know why I didn't get a hundred, and if I told her Heather Rubin had a new boyfriend, as if I cared, she'd ask me why I didn't try to make myself more attractive to boys, as if she wouldn't get totally weird if some boy actually did like me. She was certainly the last person I wanted to talk to about what was going on with Mr. P.

But that's who Mom was talking about when I went back downstairs. "I'll talk to you when I get home from parents' night, Ma. . . . No, at the junior high. I want to take a good look at this Mr. Padovano. . . . Yeah, that's the one. It's all over town that he's gay. . . . So I'm concerned, Ma. I'm not crazy about the idea that this teacher might be gay. . . . Because Janice worships him, Mother, and I don't want her to think that being gay is something wonderful. . . . I don't want to talk about it now, Ma. I'll call you when we get home." God, please, Mom, get a job.

Daddy actually came home in time to go to school too, and they left about seven-thirty, leaving me scared to death that Mom was going to say something embarrassing to Mr. P. I was doing my geometry homework and eating ice cream in the kitchen when they got home, and my ears pricked up right away when I heard them by the coat closet.

". . . seems like a nice enough fella to me," Daddy said.

"I mean do you think he looks gay?" Mom asked.

"I don't know," Daddy said. "He isn't swishy, if that's

66

what you mean." He headed to the kitchen, Mom trailing after him. "When did all this come up?"

"I don't know, I heard about it last week," Mom said. "Someone vandalized his car, something like that."

Daddy saw my dish of ice cream and said, "Hey, that looks good." He opened the freezer and got the carton out.

"Neither of you needs that ice cream," Mom said.

"You're absolutely right," Daddy said. "Gimme a spoon, will ya, Jan?" I grinned and handed him a spoon from the drawer while Mom sighed.

"You know, Mr. P's car got vandalized a long time ago," I said. "Some creep spray-painted *FAGGOT* on it the day you came to school to pick me up early for the dentist, Mom. Remember I wanted to go back into school? I wanted to tell Mr. P about his car. That's the whole case for Mr. P's being gay, some idiot with a spray can."

"Did you see who did it?" Daddy asked.

"No," I lied. "I wish everybody would just forget about it. Who cares if he's gay or not? He's a great teacher, that's all I care about."

"When you're a parent, you'll understand our concern," Mom said.

"When I'm a parent, I'll judge my children's teachers by how well they teach, not by stupid gossip about their personal lives," I retorted.

"That's enough, Janice," Mom snapped.

Okay, okay. "So how am I doing in school? Am I passing everything?"

Mom gave me a *very-funny* look. I don't even know

67

why they bother going; my teachers have been giving them the same report since I was in kindergarten. "Let me see if I can get this right," Daddy said. "They said you're a . . . oh, what's the word they used? Oh, yeah, excellent. They said you're an excellent student. Except for the one who said you're outstanding."

"Thanks," I said. "I guess that's nice to hear."

"It is," Daddy said.

Mom nodded and took a spoonful of ice cream out of the carton with my spoon. "Oh, yeah," she said, remembering something. "Janice, you didn't tell me there's a big dance next week. I saw posters for it all over the school."

❧ 9 ❧

Up till then, believe it or not, I had never been to a dance, and I wasn't in any big hurry to start. I skip the Fall Harvest Dance they have for the junior youth group at temple every October, and the after-school dances they have in the gym every few Fridays. Think about it—who was gonna dance with me? I was taller and heavier than almost every boy except some of the jocks, and all of them thought of me as being from the nonhuman animal kingdom: either Baby Huey or something that has to be walked twice a day and fed Alpo. I'd seen enough dances on TV shows and in movies to know what happens to girls like me. Standing against a wall drinking Hawaiian Punch and watching girls like Heather Rubin dance all evening is not my idea of fun.

But Mom went on and on about how it was about time I started going to dances and how I could wear the new outfit she got me for my birthday, which was very pretty but too dressy to wear anywhere remotely involving school. I told her I didn't think I'd have a good time, but she acted like this was some crucial milestone in my development as a teenager, so I told her I wasn't going to pay for the ticket out of my allowance, and she said she'd give me the money, which left me out of arguments.

The next morning Holly looked really excited. "Lee Farber asked me to the Winter Dance," she bubbled.

"No kidding!" I said. "Hey, that's a big deal. He's ninth-grade treasurer. How do you know him?"

"He's in my French class."

"When did he ask you?"

"He called me last night."

"That is so cool!" I said. "Your first date in West River. I can't believe it took so long." I mean it really is pretty bizarre. But then she's fifteen already, so the ninth-grade boys are too immature for her (and for everybody else, of course), and the few who aren't are intimidated by her brains.

Holly waved to Lee in the cafeteria during lunch. "He's really nice," she said.

"Yeah, he is," I said. Sort of cute, too. Tallish and thin, curly brown hair, no zits. He smiled and waved at Holly, which was nice, because some guys are too cool to do that. "Do you want to sit with him?" I asked.

"Oh, no," she said. "He's got his own crowd to sit with."

"Maybe he wants you to join him."

"No, he'd have waved me over. I don't want to barge in unless he asks me."

We sat down and started eating. "My mom's nagging me to go to the dance," I said.

"Oh, yeah?" Holly said. "What are you gonna wear?"

"What do you mean? I'm not going," I said.

"Why not? It might be fun."

"Sure, for you," I said. "I don't wanna go without a date."

"Maybe Lee can get someone to take you," Holly said.

"He'd have to rob a bank for a big enough bribe," I said.

"Oh, stop it," Holly said. "You ought to go, Jan. It would be a good experience for you."

"You sound like my mother," I said. "She says it's about time I started to do stuff like go to dances."

"I hate to say it, but she has a point," Holly said. "Come on, it'll be okay. We'll figure out exactly what to wear, and you'll have dinner at my house before the dance, and we'll work on your makeup. You'll look terrific. You'll have a great time."

"Well, maybe," I said. It's hard to argue with someone who's all caught up in young love, or young like, or whatever was making her so happy. Between Holly and my mother, I was trapped.

Finding something for me to wear was a big challenge. "No, not a dress," Holly said. "More like an I'm-really-too-cool-to-be-here-but-I'm-doing-you-all-a-big-favor look. You know, a little weird, but in a cool way."

"People already think I look a little weird," I said. "I just want to look like everybody else." Holly gave me a get-real look. "Well, this is why I don't want to go," I continued. "It's gonna be bad enough, nobody dancing

71

with me, without everybody pointing and saying how strange I'm dressed."

"It'll be better than you standing around looking like Little Bo-Peep in that stuff your mom picks out for you. Come on, Jan, trust me."

Holly had me wear black tights, little black boots she made me get on our first trip to the mall together, and a humongous purple shirt from the store for tall and fat guys. I already knew about that place because my dad, who's moderately tall and fat, gets stuff there sometimes, but this shirt was a triple-extralarge tall, which means it's made for somebody who's about six feet six and weighs four hundred pounds. It was big even on me.

Of course there was no way my mother was gonna think that was suitable clothing for the biggest school dance of the season, so I put the shirt on a hanger under one of my stupid dresses and put the other stuff in a plastic bag and told her I would change at Holly's. "She's gonna show me some makeup," I said.

"Not too much, please," Mom said. "I don't want you looking like a fourteen-year-old hooker. You got money?"

"Yeah," I said.

"Call if you need me," she said. "I'll be home."

Holly had me put on the clothes and gave me a belt of her dad's. "Make it a little bigger than your waist," she said. Then she poofed out the shirt over the belt. If you didn't know better, you might think I actually had a bust under the shirt, and it was long enough so it looked like a short dress with a strange hem. "See, your legs aren't bad," Holly said, "and this kind of thing makes your top look bigger and your bottom look smaller."

Then she went to work on my face. Holly had told me to bring my mom's eyeliner and mascara, since she's blonde and hers would be too light. She made up my eyes mostly and put two kinds of blusher on my cheeks. When she was done, my eyes looked bigger and I looked older. "You should get some of this stuff and wear it every day," Holly said. "It really makes a difference."

"Yeah, but it doesn't look like me," I said. "Anyway, who can see it when I put on my glasses?"

"Don't wear your glasses at the dance," Holly said.

"Oh, right, that'll be very entertaining, standing around all evening watching a total blur," I said.

"You're not that nearsighted," she said. "And who says you'll just be standing around?"

"Every neuron in my brain and every fat cell under this weird shirt," I said. A car honked outside.

"Come one, that's Lee's dad," Holly said. "I want you to say out loud right now, 'I look great and I'm gonna have a great time.' "

"I look great and I'm gonna have a great time," I said.

Holly frowned. "Now say it like you mean it, Janice."

The first part of the evening wasn't so bad. Lee was very friendly and didn't act P.O.'d that I was along for the ride. His dad said, "You mean I get to chauffeur *two* beautiful women?" which was stupid, of course, but nice of him to say. The school gym was decorated with a ski theme, with piles of white fluffy stuff sprinkled with glitter draped over the equipment, and ski posters everywhere. They even managed to control the sweaty-armpit atmosphere somehow.

The teachers standing around were a little more dressed up than usual, wearing expressions ranging from "Isn't this fun?" to "The principal made me be here." Mr. P was pouring punch in a corner away from the deejay. He was wearing a suit, which was much more dressed up than usual, because in class he wears turtlenecks and plain sweaters, never anything with a tie. He looked even cuter than usual and seemed to be flirting with Ms. Christie, who teaches P.E. She was standing by the wall near the punch table along with a bunch of girls, as if she were one of them and they were all waiting for someone to ask them to dance. Probably Ms. Christie was hoping Mr. P would ask her.

The deejay, a high school kid, was playing something loud and fast that I'd heard on the radio about fifty thousand times. Half the kids in the room were dancing and the other half were milling around checking one another out. I immediately wanted to go home.

We dumped our coats, and Holly and Lee cut through the crowd to where the dancers were. I was all ready to shrink back against the wall, but Holly dragged me right up to within ten feet of the deejay. "Take your glasses off!" she yelled as she and Lee started dancing.

I did, but not before taking a quick look around the immediate area to see if there was anyone I knew. Rachel Strauss and some other girls from youth group were nearby, so I went over to them and we all said hi.

"You look nice," Rachel said. I couldn't tell if she was more surprised just to see me at a dance or at the fact that I was wearing makeup and no glasses.

"Is anyone asking anyone to dance, or did you have to come with someone?" I asked.

"Stacy danced," Rachel said.

"With Eric Chang," Stacy Milstein said. "He's over there—he's dancing with a lot of people."

"We just got here a little while ago," Rachel said.

I stood there with them for what seemed like hours. Every so often guys would cruise by and check out our little group. Eric Chang asked Rachel to dance once, and Laurie Weiss danced with two different guys, and Stacy, who's known far and wide as an airhead but has a big chest, got asked to dance a lot. Some boys from our classes came over and talked to us and acted friendly enough, but they didn't ask us to dance or even if any of us wanted to get some punch.

After a while I saw Mr. P at the edge of the crowd around the dancers. I couldn't see him too well without my glasses, but I could tell it was him from his hair and his gray suit. Several times some guy would come up to him and say something, and Mr. P would shake his head and the guy would move away. That happened with at least three different boys. I listened to song after song, getting bored, with a headache starting between my eyes. Meanwhile, all the popular girls like Heather Rubin and Felicia Rim never left the dance floor (and never seemed to get sweaty, either), and Holly looked like she was having a great time with Lee.

The deejay put on a slow song, and the dancers thinned out some. During the previous slow song,

Holly and Lee had come over and chatted with Rachel and me, but now Lee took Holly in his arms and they started to sway with the music, looking very romantic. A lump formed in my throat, and suddenly I realized that I was the tallest girl in the gym and probably looked like a ridiculous purple elephant. "I'm gonna get some punch," I said to Rachel.

It's not that I wanted any of those guys to be my boyfriend or even that I wanted to dance, since I knew I'd look completely comical if I tried, and everyone would make fun of me. I just felt like, what am I doing here? This isn't where I'm supposed to be. I'm supposed to be home, watching TV or reading a book.

I went to the punch corner, which was darker than the dance floor, at least during the fast songs, leaned against the cool cinder block wall with the rest of the kids who just wanted to stay in the shadows, and put on my glasses. Ms. Christie was pouring punch now, but Mr. P came back and asked, "Need a break?"

"Oh, no, Dennis, you've done your time," Ms. Christie said. "I don't want you to get this slop on that beautiful suit."

"I don't mind, really," Mr. P said.

"Well, maybe for five minutes," she said. "But I'll be right back."

"Take your time," he said.

I went up to the table and got some punch. "Hi, Mr. P."

"Hi, Janice," he said, looking really happy to see me. "Hey, you look terrific!"

"So do you," I said. "You should dress like that for school."

"Nah, it's bad for faculty morale, making your colleagues look like slobs," he said. I giggled. "Actually I have only one good suit, so I have to save it for special occasions," he continued.

"You call this a special occasion, Mr. P?" I said disparagingly.

"I think so, for a lot of people anyway. You must have thought so earlier this evening," he said, touching his face.

"The makeup is Holly's work," I said. "I wouldn't be here if Holly and my mom hadn't nagged me."

"Not having a good time?"

"No, not that I expected to. I mean, I didn't think anyone would ask me to dance, but I'd never been to a dance before, and I thought it would at least be interesting. You know, different stuff to look at, people acting different than they do all day at school. Instead I've got Holly yelling at me not to wear my glasses and everybody hanging around acting the same way they always do, except at a dance it's all set to music."

Mr. P widened his eyes with fake enthusiasm. "But Janice, it's such *great music*, and the deejay's doing such a *great job*," he said, making me giggle again.

Just then a guy and a girl came by holding hands. "You want some punch?" the guy asked her.

The girl was about to take some, then she saw Mr. P behind the table and took her hand away, her face all nervous. "Uh, no," she said. "Maybe later."

Even in that dim corner of the room, I could see the red move up Mr. P's face from his white shirt collar. At that moment Ms. Christie came back and started chatting up Mr. P a mile a minute. I moved off a little way,

77

totally mortified for him. How could that girl be so stupid, acting like Mr. P had AIDS and could give it to her by pouring punch? I watched him talk to Ms. Christie, amazed at how he could just snap back and act so normal and friendly. If something like that happened to me, I'd go through the floor.

Suddenly I was startled by a tap on my shoulder. It was Lee. "Would you like to dance?" he asked.

"Oh, that's okay," I said. "We don't have to."

"No, come on," he said in a friendly way. What a nice guy! No wonder Holly liked him.

"Really, I don't want to right now. I kind of have a headache. But thanks a lot for asking me," I said sincerely.

"Okay," Lee said. "See ya later." I watched him go back toward Holly.

Then Mr. P came over to me. "Didn't you want to dance with him?"

"Oh, that's Holly's date," I said. "He didn't really want to dance with me. Holly must have told him to come over here and ask me."

"Are you sure?" he asked. "Maybe he really wanted to."

I pointed toward the dance area. "Mr. P, look, he's reporting back to Holly. 'I asked her, Holly, but she said she had a headache,'" I mimicked.

"Well, then, you're free for this dance. Shall we?" Mr. P invited.

No way! That had to be breaking some kind of rule. "Oh, uh, I don't think so, Mr. P," I stammered. "I can't really dance."

"Oh, sure you can, everybody can dance," he said.

"Just move back and forth to the music." He started to move his arms from side to side. I felt embarrassed and fascinated at the same time.

"Mr. P, I really can't," I said, feeling like I was rooted to the floor.

"You mean to tell me you have never moved your body in rhythm to a musical beat?" he asked. He was moving his feet now, too.

"Well, yeah, in my room."

"Well, just pretend you're in your room now. Come on, it's fun." I sort of swished my arms from side to side, but Mr. P wasn't satisfied. "Come on, move your feet. Right foot first, step up, step back." He moved forward and back to the beat, in two little tracks. I tried it; it wasn't too hard. "Now make your hips go with your feet. Put your whole body into it." He danced with a little more swagger and looked more like a college guy than a teacher. I could feel the chubby parts of my body shake when I did what Mr. P said, but it was dark back there, and I didn't think anyone was noticing us. "All right, you're dancing!" Mr. P yelled. "Move your arms, too!" I just did what he did, and after a while, it was really fun!

We danced till the end of the song, and when it was over, Mr. P took out a handkerchief and mopped his forehead. "What a workout!" he said. "I'm getting old. I used to be able to do that for hours."

"You didn't *look* old," I said. The deejay said, "And now for another spot of romance in our evening together," and he put on a slow song.

"That's more my speed right now," Mr. P said. "Want to try a slow one?"

"Oh, no," I said, smiling but horrified. I was all sweaty and had no idea how to slow-dance. Mr. P would think I was not only a klutz but totally gross.

"Come on, it's not hard," he said. He came up to me and took my right hand in his left one and put my other hand on his shoulder. Then he put his right hand on my waist. "Now, when I move my left foot, you move your right foot in the same direction, and vice versa, and just follow me around that way. Try not to look at your feet." I immediately looked at my feet.

"This is so weird," I said.

"It is, until you get used to it. Don't your parents dance?"

"Not really. On special occasions, I guess."

"Oh, I grew up watching my parents dance," Mr. P said. "They still put on records and dance in the living room. They met at a dance hall, must be forty years ago."

"That's so sweet," I said. "No wonder you dance so great."

"Thank you," he said. "So how do you think practice is going?"

"Okay, I guess." I was concentrating on not tripping over Mr. P's feet.

Just then this big kid I didn't know who looked like a total wise-ass creep came over to us and said, "Hey, can I have a turn?"

I looked at Mr. P and shook my head a little. Mr. P smiled and said, "Maybe Janice will let you have the next dance."

The guy's face got even creepier. "But I wanna dance with *you*, Mr. Padovano."

Mr. P's face tightened, but he kept a little smile fixed. "I don't think so."

"Oh, please, Mr. Padovano? I've been waiting all night to ask you."

Mr. P's voice took on a hard edge. "I'm sure there are any number of boys who'd be thrilled to dance with you," he said. "Would you excuse us, please?"

The creep moved away. "You're breakin' my heart, Mr. Padovano!" he called over his shoulder.

Mr. P let go of me then. We had been dancing near the punch, and suddenly he brought his fist down onto the table, a short, hard hit that you couldn't even hear over the music. But one of the cups of punch jumped off the table and spilled all over one leg of Mr. P's suit. His face twisted with anger, and for a second I thought he was going to knock a bunch more cups off the table out of plain rage, but then he sighed and looked around for some napkins. I saw some at the other end of the table and handed them to him.

"Thanks, Janice," he said, mopping off his pants leg. "Did I get you?"

"Uh-uh," I said. Mr. P glanced around the gym with kind of a nervous look, and I realized at that moment that the other boys I'd seen go up to him earlier had also asked him to dance.

But then he threw the napkins into a trash can and held up his arms. "Shall we continue?" he asked.

"I don't know," I said. I felt awful for him, and I was sweatier than ever.

"Are you uncomfortable?" he asked.

"Not from dancing with you," I said. "I'm just mad at that guy."

"Let's not let him spoil all our fun," Mr. P said. He smiled at me reassuringly, and we kept dancing. Then, behind me, I heard the same creep say, "Sure he's queer. Look what he's dancing with!"

I froze in place. My feet just wouldn't move anymore. Now Mr. P *really* looked angry. "Forget about it," he said to me quietly.

"I think it's time for me to go home," I said.

Mr. P squeezed my hand understandingly. "Are you sure?" he said.

"Yeah."

"Do you need a ride?"

"No, I'll call my mom. I have to tell Holly, 'cause I came with her."

"Okay, then I'll see you Monday," Mr. P said. "You sure you're okay?"

"Oh, yeah," I said. "Bye, Mr. P. Thanks for the dances."

"It was my pleasure," he said.

I was trying not to cry by the time I got to Holly and Lee. "I really have a terrible headache, so I'm gonna call my mom to come get me," I said.

"Seriously?" Holly said. Actually by that time it was true.

"Yeah," I said. "Remember that next time you don't want me to wear my glasses."

"You want us to wait outside with you?" Lee asked.

"No, I'll be fine."

I dug out my coat, called Mom from the pay phone outside the gym, and waited by the entrance (with a few other kids who'd given up on having a good time) until I saw her station wagon. I got her to leave me alone in the car by telling her my head was pounding, but as soon as we got in the house, she noticed the collar of the purple shirt sticking out from my coat, and when she saw Holly's handiwork, she threw a major hissy fit. "I didn't wear that much makeup at my wedding," she yelled. "You look like a zombie from Mars."

The perfect end to a perfect evening.

❧ 10 ❧

The Tuesday after the dance, the local newspaper had an article on page 12 with the headline *Gay Teacher Dismissed in Shawegun*. Some school district upstate had found out an elementary teacher was gay and fired him. A few days later, the paper printed this letter:

> I am heartened to learn that a school district in this state has had the probity and intelligence to weed out a teacher who presents a clear danger to the moral and physical health of its students. Our local school boards would do well to take a hard look at the faculty members in our neighborhood schools and follow Shawegun's example if necessary. Our children have enough negative influences from television, movies, and rock music without the daily example of a degenerate lifestyle confronting them in the classroom.
>
> Susan Grainger
> West River

My first thought was, how stupid can you get? This was the same kind of nasty, prejudiced thing Kevin was always saying, only in fancier language. Then I looked at the letter writer's name and town and felt sort of scared.

The next day at lunch, Holly and I went up to Cory Grainger and asked him if his mom had written that letter. "Yeah, that was my mom," he said, sounding ashamed.

"God, how nasty," I said. "She meant Mr. P, didn't she?"

"What a sucky attitude," Holly said. "No offense to your mom."

"You don't feel that way, do you?" I asked.

"Of course not," Cory said. "I had Mr. P last year. I think he's great. My parents are just real religious, you know? Our minister is always preaching about how it's against the Bible to be gay. I think it's stupid, but I can't do anything about it."

"Well, as long as *you* don't believe it, I guess it doesn't matter what your parents think," Holly said.

Cory looked very uncomfortable. "It does sort of matter," he said. "They're making me quit the All-Stars."

"What!" we both yelled. "But we need you on the team!" I said.

"Yeah, tell them they're wrong," Holly said.

"It's pretty impossible to convince my parents that they're wrong about anything," Cory said, his mouth twisting in a strange way. "I can't fight them. They'd make my life miserable. You don't know how they can be."

How? I wanted to ask. But something in Cory's face made me not ask. I imagined his parents making him get on his knees and pray for hours instead of letting him eat dinner or watch TV. Or maybe they hit him. "Are you sure you can't change your mind?" I asked.

"It's not something I get to decide," he said sadly, moving off. He quit right after school that day.

At the end of the week, Mr. P said at practice, "Mr. Perlman says that with Cory gone, we're a little shaky in math. Kevin, he says you *could* be further along if you tried a little harder."

"I'm doing my best, Mr. Padovano, but the keys on that calculator you loaned me are just too damn small," he said. Shawn and Ron laughed while Holly and I just rolled our eyes at each other.

"Mr. Perlman seemed to think you were hanging back in your pursuit of the elusive x," Mr. P said good-humoredly.

"Well, sorry, but I haven't been through the Nerd Factory assembly line," Kevin said. "We're still pushing around decimal points in Math 9."

"Well, then, we'll get you a little extra help," Mr. P said. "Would any of you be willing to help Kevin this weekend?"

No volunteers. Karen and Sheila looked like they were trying to make themselves invisible. "I wouldn't mind some private tutoring from Johansen," Kevin said, leering.

Holly didn't *quite* go "Eeeuuu." I leaned over and whispered in her ear, "If you'll help him, I'll go too."

She thought for a second. "I'll tutor him if Janice comes too."

Kevin's face fell, but Mr. P looked pleased. "Wonderful! When can you all get together?"

Holly shrugged. "Saturday afternoon?"

Kevin shook his head. "I'm gonna be in the city."

"Really?" I said enviously. "Are you gonna see a play?"

"Nah, just hang around with my brother. He lives there," Kevin said.

"How about Sunday?" Holly said. We agreed to meet at Kevin's house on Sunday afternoon.

Holly's mom picked me up Sunday, and on the way to Kevin's house, Holly told me about her date with Lee Saturday night—a horror movie and pizza afterwards. As soon as we got out of the car, Holly told me that Lee had kissed her for the first time, in front of her house at the end of the date. "Wasn't his mom or dad right there in the car?" I asked.

"You know the bushes next to our front door?" she said. I nodded. "Well, if you get between them and the wall, whoever's in the driveway can't see you."

I nodded again. She looked really happy and embarrassed at the same time, like she wanted to tell me more but didn't know how. "Um, was it nice?"

"Yeah," Holly said, still smiling.

I wasn't sure how much more I wanted to know. "Uh . . ." I shrugged. "Were tongues involved?"

She got totally red, which is always funny to watch. "Janice!" she said.

"Well, you looked like you wanted to tell me," I said.

"God," Holly said. Then, going up Kevin's front walk, she hissed, "*Yes.*"

"Oh," I said. "Well, congratulations, I guess." I rang

Kevin's doorbell, wondering what it would feel like to have some guy's tongue in my mouth.

Kevin's mother answered the door and looked completely surprised to see *two* girls, one of them blonde and cute, coming to see Kevin. "Kevin, your friends are here," she called downstairs. "Send 'em down," we heard him yell from the depths.

Holly looked intrigued and disgusted at the same time as she took in the grunginess and the interesting decorations in Kevin's room. His mother called down, "Kevin, wouldn't your friends like some refreshments?"

"They're not my friends," he yelled back. Holly made a face at me like, how typical. "You want anything?" he said ungraciously.

"I wouldn't mind a soda," Holly said, I think just to make him act like a host. Kevin sighed and clumped up the stairs.

"God, this room is gross," she said. She started to pull up the cover of the unmade bed, since the two of us would have to sit on it, and saw the corner of a magazine under the covers. When she pulled it out, it was a *Penthouse*. "Oh, yuck!" she said.

"I'm sure he just reads it for the articles," I said, and we both giggled. We sat on the bed and turned a few pages. The pictures of naked women confused me. I knew the whole idea of putting sexy pictures of women in magazines for guys to look at was sexist and nasty, and a woman who posed for those pictures was just selling her body. But at the same time I kind of envied any woman who felt so comfortable about her body that she could take off her clothes and show it to thousands of people. The women in the magazine were so pretty. I wondered if I could ever get my body to look like that. Maybe in a zillion years, provided I ever grew breasts, of course. "What a slob," I said. "These two pages are stuck together. He must've spilled soda on them."

Holly looked at the stuck-together pages, went red again, and started half-laughing, half-choking. "What's so funny?" I said.

"Well . . ." she said. Then we heard Kevin's footsteps on the stairs and quickly shoved the magazine back under the covers. Kevin came in with some sodas and a bowl of pretzels, which he practically threw at us.

"Thanks," I said, opening a can of soda. "Did you have fun yesterday with your brother?"

"Yeah, it was okay," Kevin said. "We went to an art gallery, and then we had lunch, and then we mostly hung around his place and listened to music."

"*You* went to an art gallery?" Holly said.

"Yeah, blondie, I went to an art gallery," he said. "I've spent a lot more time looking at art than you have, unless you count all the cow pies up where you come from as works of art."

"Sorry," Holly said, looking very much put in her place.

"What kind of art?" I asked.

"Some of it was abstract paintings, and there were some metal sculptures."

"Abstract, you mean the kind that looks like the guy just threw paint at the wall?" I said.

"You're showing your ignorance, nerdo," Kevin said. "Just because a painting isn't some B.S. landscape doesn't mean it isn't saying something."

"I saw a movie on cable that showed an abstract artist working, and it looked like he planned everything very carefully," Holly said.

"Damn right," Kevin said. "The guy who did these paintings is a friend of my brother's, and last summer he took me over to his studio, and the guy was working on some of the paintings that were in the gallery yesterday. You better believe it takes planning."

"Wow," I said. "You got to see that stuff before it was finished?"

"Yeah," Kevin said, sounding a little proud.

"That's pretty cool," Holly said.

"Where does your brother live?" I asked.

"Greenwich Village," Kevin said.

"Oh, I've always wanted to walk around there," I said. "I've only been in midtown Manhattan—theaters and stores and my dad's office."

"It's nice there," Kevin said neutrally.

"Did your brother get you interested in music from the sixties?" I asked.

"Yeah, he's really into that stuff," Kevin said. "He used to play in a rock band when he was in college. He's a really good guitarist. He's teaching me how to play." For the first time, Kevin sounded friendly and enthusiastic. "You should see his record collection. He's really taught me a lot."

"You're lucky," I said. "All my little sister is interested in is who's on 'Donahue.' "

Kevin's face sort of frosted over, like he'd caught himself being friendly and didn't like it. "Well, we better study," he said.

I mostly worked on practice problems by myself while Holly led Kevin through some word problems and simple stuff with variables. Every so often, when Kevin was bent over a problem, Holly would gaze around the room, picking up some new detail of the decor, and every so often when Holly was looking at her notebook and explaining something, Kevin would sneak this little look at her, like he couldn't believe someone as pretty as Holly was sitting on his bed and he sure would like to ask her out.

Not in your wildest dreams, tubbo, I thought. Kevin had asked a girl to go to the Winter Dance with him—it was by the lockers and I overheard—and she'd turned him down cold. She wasn't anything like Holly, just a very ordinary-looking eighth-grader, a little heavy on the eye makeup, and she'd said no, thanks, in a voice that was more like no thanks, I'll hold out for someone less fat and obnoxious. I almost felt a little sorry for Kevin that day, especially since he'd asked sort of nicely. In fact, at times he showed fleeting signs of turning into something resembling a human being. Maybe if he kept hanging out with his brother, who appeared to be a good cultural influence, anyway.

At four o'clock, Holly got up. "Well, I think you've got it a lot more than you did before," she said. "Janice, we better go."

I stood up and Kevin did too. "Uh, thanks," he said. "You sure you don't want another soda?"

"No, Janice and I have to study for tomorrow's test. You too, I guess."

Kevin had in fact transferred into our geography class, where he answered Mr. P's questions as sarcastically as possible without actually being rude—and aced every assignment.

"What test?" Kevin asked.

"We've got a test in period six tomorrow," I said impatiently. "On Africa."

"Oh, yeah," Kevin said. "What's to study? The Pygmies are short, the Watusi are tall, and apartheid sucked, right?"

"I think Mr. P's gonna go into a little more depth than that," Holly said.

"Whatever," Kevin said. "I'm just happy we're finally leaving the Dark Continent. I was getting tired of Todd Ginsburg telling us how we're all descended from Africans. If that's the case, how come I get sunburned so easy?"

Kevin got a ninety-six on the test, three points higher than he got on the Southeast Asia test. I got a ninety-two.

Kim's birthday is just before Valentine's Day. She had a dental appointment in White Plains, and while she was getting her teeth cleaned, Mom and I ran into Macy's so I could get her a birthday present. I bought Kim two pairs of dangly, beaded earrings, which my mother thought were ugly but I assured her were the height of fashion among eleven-year-olds. We were walking out of the store through the men's department when Mom said, "Wait, they have wallets on sale, and your father's is falling apart."

She started looking through the wallets marked SAVE 34%. I started to do a little people watching and suddenly saw Mr. Padovano at the men's sweater counter, around a corner not ten feet away. I knew he lived somewhere in Westchester County because he'd told us he commuted across the river, but it was still weird seeing him in the middle of Macy's. I was about to go over to him when I noticed another guy was with him—a dark guy about Mr. P's height but a little older, with a round face and a heavier build. They were holding sweaters up to each other, not seriously, kind of fooling around.

"Purple is just not your color," Mr. P said to his friend. He picked up another sweater. "How about a cardigan?"

"Dennis, please, I'm not that old," the other guy said. "Oh, I like this one." He turned his back to me and picked up a green sweater with a bunch of blue and gold and maroon swirls knitted into it. "Here, your students will go wild."

Mr. P looked at the sweater in the mirror. "My students will decide only queers wear sweaters like this," he said. "It *is* nice." He looked at the price tag and made a face. "Oh, please, Paul, it costs a fortune," he said, starting to put the sweater away.

"But it's gorgeous," the other guy said. "Come on, splurge a little."

"It's not like I don't have plenty of sweaters," Mr. P said.

"Well, that's true," his friend said. "They've practically taken over the apartment." He put the sweater down. "All I can say is, don't be surprised to find it next to your birthday cake." Mr. P smiled at him just the way a guy in the movies smiles at a girl he's in love with.

Oh, God.

Mr. P must have felt me staring at him, because he looked over his friend's shoulder and saw me. He got a very scared look, so scared that I wanted to run to him and say I didn't care, it didn't matter to me if he had a boyfriend. I smiled and waved at him, like hi, I understand if you don't want to talk to me with your friend there and my mother here. I was hoping the scared look would go away when I did that, but it didn't. Then I glanced at my mother. She was standing next to me with a little Macy's bag in her hand, looking right at Mr. P and his friend, and I thought, oh, God, all over again.

"What are you looking at?" Mr. P's friend asked.

"One of my students," he said, his face going back to normal. "One of my favorite students, in fact," he said a little louder. He and his friend came over to us. "Hi, Janice," Mr. P said.

"Hi, Mr. P."

"Paul, this is Janice Green, one of my best honors students, and her mom. Janice, Mrs. Green, this is my friend Paul Goldsmith."

"Hi," I said, shaking hands with Paul. Mom gave Paul a cold little smile and shook hands too.

"What brings you across the river?" Mr. P asked.

"My sister's at the dentist," I said. "I just got her a birthday present."

"Oh, yeah?" Mr. P said. "What did you get her?"

"Earrings, you know, the big kind eleven-year-olds like."

"Sounds perfect," he said. "Well, now you know what I do in my spare time. Some men go bowling, some watch TV, I hang around Macy's."

"As long as it keeps you off the streets," I said. Mr. P smiled, and Paul laughed out loud, as if he

94

hadn't expected me to come up with that particular remark.

"Janice, we have to get your sister," Mom said.

"Okay," I said. "Bye, Mr. Goldsmith. See ya Monday, Mr. P."

"Yup," he said. "Bye, Mrs. Green."

Paul said nice-to-meet-you, and we went out toward the parking garage. Mom's mouth was locked up in a tight, thin line.

❧ 11 ❧

Mom kept up a frosty silence all the way to the car. Maybe if I bring it up first, she can see how unimportant it is, I thought. "Gee, I guess the rumors about Mr. P are true," I said lightly as Mom pulled out of the parking lot.

"I want you off that team," she said grimly. "Maybe I can get you transferred into another social studies class."

So much for the offhand approach. "Forget it!" I said. "I'm not leaving the team. We already lost Cory."

"I simply don't want you in contact with someone like that," she said. "I don't like the idea of him being around kids at all."

"Mom, that's crazy. Mr. P wouldn't do anything to hurt us. He certainly isn't gonna give us AIDS, if that's what you're worried about."

"How do you know?" she asked.

Oh, please. "Because the only way you can get AIDS is to have sex with someone who has it or use the same needle for sharing drugs or mix some of his blood with yours. You know that, Mom."

"You can't be too careful, Janice."

"Okay, Mom," I said. "I promise not to have sex with Mr. P or share needles with him or get a blood transfusion from him. That's assuming he even has AIDS, which I bet he doesn't."

"Don't make light of this, Janice," Mom said. "Gay people don't belong in schools."

"Why not?"

Mom searched for words for a moment. "They're not good role models."

I twisted around in the seat, wishing I could scream. "Mom, don't you realize how dumb you sound?"

"Don't talk to me like that, Janice."

"You make it sound like he's gonna try to turn us all gay, and that's just st—" I was going to say *stupid*, but that would just make her madder. "That's silly."

"Janice, he's someone you're in contact with every day, and from what you and others say, he's very popular."

"Of course he's popular, he's a great teacher!"

"That's beside the point," Mom said. "If you know he's gay, and you like him, that's like saying there's nothing wrong with being a homosexual."

"It is not, and there *isn't* anything wrong with it!" I exploded. "It's just part of who he is! He has brown hair, he wears sweaters, he's gay! So what?"

"It just isn't right, it isn't normal," Mom said.

"Says who?"

"Janice, I don't want to discuss this anymore," she said. "When you're older, you'll realize that I'm right."

"When I'm older, I plan to be a lot more accepting

of people than you are," I said. Mom gave me an angry look but said nothing. "How do you know so much about gay people anyway? The only gay man you know is Billy." Billy cuts our hair. He's very feminine.

"I've known other gays, Janice."

"Where?"

"In college," she said. "And being a homosexual is very different from having brown hair or wearing sweaters."

"How?" I asked.

She hesitated. "It just is," she said. "It isn't normal. It's unnatural."

"Well, I'm about six inches taller than the average fourteen-year-old girl," I said. "Does that make me abnormal and unnatural?"

"You're talking about two totally different things," Mom said.

"No, I'm not," I said. "Being straight or gay is something you're born with, just like if you're gonna be tall or short."

"Who told you that, Mr. Padovano?"

"No," I said. "I've read it in about sixteen different magazines."

"Well, I would rather protect my children than take a chance they'll be influenced by a deviant role model."

"Who's your idea of a good role model?" I said.

"Your father and I try to set a good example," Mom said.

I looked at her incredulously. "You and Daddy? Come on!"

Mom looked very insulted. "What's wrong with Daddy and me?"

"Nothing, you're good parents, but I don't especially want to be like either of you. He works such long hours I hardly ever see him, and all you do is drive us around and go shopping."

We were stopped at a red light, and Mom turned toward me, looking so mad she was practically growing fangs. "How dare you talk about us like that? Your father and I work very hard to give you girls a beautiful home and everything you could possibly need!"

"What I need is a mother who doesn't make stupid judgments all the time!"

Mom took her right hand off the steering wheel and smacked me right in the face. It was a short smack and didn't hurt much, but it was pretty shocking, since she hardly ever hits me. "You listen to me, young lady. You are off that team, and if I hear one more word out of you, you can forget about TV and telephone privileges for the rest of the month."

Well, that was about all I had to say, anyway. I got in the backseat when we picked up Kim, who filled the conversational gap the rest of the way home.

That was Saturday. I wasn't too talkative when Holly called Sunday and gave me her weekly date-with-Lee report (more tongues, yuck), and on Monday I could barely face her or anybody else. "What's wrong with you, anyway?" she asked at lunch, watching me pick little pieces off my tuna sandwich.

"Uh, I feel crummy," I said truthfully enough.

"Did you get your period?" she asked.

"Nah," I said.

"Then what is it?"

"I'm all right, I just don't feel great," I said.

It was lame, but at least it gave me an idea for how to weasel out of practice. "Mr. P, would it be okay if I didn't stay for practice today?" I asked after period six. "I don't feel too good."

"She didn't feel good at lunch," Holly corroborated.

"Can't hold out, huh?" Mr. P said. "Sure, no problem. We've got only a few weeks to go, gotta keep you healthy."

"Thanks, Mr. P," I said. "I'll be okay tomorrow." He gave me a worksheet about *Pudd'nhead Wilson* and I caught the regular bus home.

Daddy wasn't home for dinner (for a change), so it was just Kim, Mom, and me. "Did you tell Mr. Padovano you were quitting?" Mom asked.

"Sort of," I said.

"What do you mean, sort of? You either did or you didn't," Mom said.

"You're quitting the All-Stars? Why?" Kim asked.

"You want to answer that one, Mom?" I said sarcastically.

"Janice felt she was taking on too much work with the All-Stars, and she was afraid her grades were going to go down," Mom said smoothly. God, what a liar. She'd probably been practicing.

"Oh," Kim said, not sounding very convinced. I left the table as soon as I could, wishing I had the guts to tell Kim the truth and tell Mom what I thought of her and her lies. But of course I didn't even have the guts to tell Mr. P and Holly and everybody else I was quitting the team. I did the worksheet Mr. P gave me, but it didn't make my conscience hurt less.

When I got on the school bus Tuesday morning, Kevin said, "Green!" as if I were his long-lost sister bringing him his half of the family millions. As soon as I sat down in my regular seat, he came thundering up the aisle and dropped himself into the seat in front of me. "You've made a miraculous recovery," he said, his voice full of fake wonder.

"Yeah, it's gonna be in all the medical journals," I said.

"So what're you gonna tell Padovano next practice?" he asked. "Cousin visiting from the old country? Senate investigation? Bubonic plague?"

"Leave me alone," I said.

"Come on, Green, I knew you were full of it, and Padovano knew it too. You better forget about a life of crime; you're a lousy liar."

"I wasn't lying. I felt bad yesterday and I wanted to go straight home."

"Uh-uh," Kevin said. "Either your folks are coming on like Grainger's, or the truth about Dennis the Menace has finally sunk in and you can't face the fact that you'll never capture his girlish heart."

"Shut up," I said. "Whatever my problem is, it's none of your business."

"*Au contraire*," he said. "If you wimp out of the Nerd-Stars, I'll be right behind you."

"No way," I said, outraged. "We had a deal."

"I don't feel any obligation to keep wasting my valuable time if you're just gonna go your merry way," Kevin said.

"I can still turn you in for painting his car, you creep," I hissed. "God, it's because of you that people like Cory's mom are all bent out of shape. Don't you feel even a little sorry?"

"Hell, if I hadn't decorated his car, somebody else would have," he said.

"How do you know?" I said, my voice rising. "How do you know anything about anything?"

"Quit babbling, Green," Kevin said. He got up and leaned over me, looking like a grizzly bear who couldn't decide whether or not I was lunch. "I may not be a straight-A Goody Two-shoes like you, but I know a lot more about faggots than you do, and I know what happens when they don't stay in their happy homo world."

"You really are a prejudiced creep," I said. "You sound just like my mom."

"Ha, I was right, your folks are making you quit," he said. "Well, just remember, the day you get the nerve to tell Tutti-Frutti the truth, all bets are off between you and me." With that, he lumbered down the aisle and crashed down in his usual spot.

The teachers had a faculty meeting after school, so there was no practice, but by suppertime my stomach was tied up in about ten knots and I still didn't know what to do. I wasn't absolutely essential to the team, since Mr. P still had Holly and Sheila on the Honors level, but if Kevin left too, West River wouldn't have enough students to compete.

The three of us ate dinner in silence, Mom's pot roast and gluey rice sitting like lead on my stomach. It was my turn to clear the table, so after we finished eating, Kim went upstairs to finish her homework and I started rinsing off plates and putting them in the dishwasher. Usually Mom settles down in front of the TV, but she started handing me silverware.

"I don't want you to think Mrs. Grainger and I are the only parents concerned about Mr. Padovano," she said. "A lot of people in the community have been talking about him."

"I'm sure they have," I said sullenly.

"Mrs. Milstein says some parents are organizing a meeting at the American Legion hall, and your principal promised to be there. I don't think he would go unless he thought there was cause for concern."

"Are you gonna go to this meeting?"

"Probably," Mom said. "I'm interested in what they have to say. Mrs. Milstein said she and a couple of other people I know are going to go."

"That's very interesting," I said. "Does this group have a name, like Parents for Fag-Bashing?"

Mom's face darkened immediately. "I don't like that kind of talk, Janice."

"What kind of talk? The word *fag* or the kind that says those people are narrow-minded and unfair?"

"That's not for you to decide, Janice."

I threw a handful of silverware into the sink and spun around. "What are you talking about?" I yelled. "Who's gonna decide for me, *you?* I'm old enough to know right from wrong, and you're wrong! Persecuting Mr. P is wrong! Making me quit the team is wrong!" Suddenly my dinner started jumping around in my stomach, and I ran past Mom and into the little bathroom next to the back door. I lifted the toilet seat and knelt down just in time before the pot roast, rice, salad, and diet Coke went into the bowl.

I flushed it down, rinsed my mouth, and went back through the kitchen. "What's the matter, are you sick?" Mom asked, stepping toward me. "Let me feel your head."

"Don't touch me," I said, backing away. It occurred to me for the very first time that I was not only bigger than my mother but big enough to push her right up against the kitchen cabinets and hold her there if I were a more violent kind of person. "Don't touch me; don't talk to me." I ran upstairs and picked up the phone in the den. If any adult could understand, Bubbie could. Please be home, please help me.

Bubbie picked up and sounded glad to hear from me. "Darling, I just got home. Let me take off my shoes"—I smiled, picturing her taking off her shoes and putting on the fuzzy slippers I got her for her birthday the year before last—"and sit down. Now what's new?"

I told her everything that was happening concerning Mr. P, including Kevin's threat to quit the team but not why he was on the team in the first place, and that I was so upset I'd just barfed up my supper. It turned out Mom had already told Bubbie about seeing Mr. P and his friend in Macy's. "I told her it wasn't such a big deal, but I guess it really bothers her," Bubbie said.

"But, Bubbie, why? Why can't she see that Mr. P couldn't possibly hurt us?"

"I don't know, darling." Bubbie sighed. "I'm sure she truly believes she's doing her best to protect you."

"But I don't need to be protected from Mr. P!" I said. "She's totally overreacting. Were you this over-protective when she was a kid?"

"No, I wasn't," Bubbie said. "In fact, your mother probably thinks I didn't protect her enough. She was very unhappy about having the only mother who worked all day, and I'm sure she thought I didn't care about her. A lot of what she does, she does to be as different from me as she can."

"Well, she's being stupid," I said. "I wish she'd be a lot more like you and a lot less like her."

"Don't say that, darling," Bubbie said. "Everything your mother does is because she loves you and Kim and wants you to be happy."

"It's not working," I said, starting to cry. "She's making me miserable. If I quit the team like she wants, I'll never be able to face anyone at school again, and if I don't quit the team, I don't know what she'll do to me."

"I'll talk to her," Bubbie said.

"Bubbie, why is she so prejudiced against gay people?"

"That I don't know," Bubbie said, sounding sincerely confused. "Your mother has always had a fear of the unusual. Maybe that's part of it. I do know one thing, though—throwing up is not good. Let me talk to her."

"Oh, thanks, Bubbie, I love you," I said. I blew her a kiss and we hung up. Ten seconds later, the phone rang. Fifteen minutes later, Mom came into my room, where I was doing math homework, and said I could stay on the team but I was not to let Mr. P drive me home anymore.

"Sure, Mom," I said. She went down to the basement to do some laundry and I went down to the kitchen for a snack. Suddenly I was famished.

❧ *12* ❧

I'd like bowling alleys a lot more if they didn't smell like cigarette butts and two-day-old socks. On the other hand, I can think of worse places to spend a rainy afternoon. My parents used to like bowling, back when my father spent enough time at home for them to do things together, and they showed me how, and unlike some girls I know, I can actually make the ball go all the way down the lane and hit some pins most of the time. Nothing makes me more annoyed than to watch a girl throw the ball into the gutter and act cute about it, which is what Heather Rubin had been doing all afternoon.

It was the Sunday before the Academic All-Stars competition, and our temple's junior youth group was having a bowling party. Holly and I went so we could take a break from studying, and of course Holly also went because Lee was going. Now everybody was finished bowling or wrapping up the last game, and dripping parents were starting to appear inside the front entrance.

Our group of four was all done—I'd been bowling with Lee, Holly, and Ron Kempner—and we'd turned in our bowling shoes and were hanging out between the shoe counter and the entrance eating the last of our french fries. Some of the parents were talking about Mr. P. The buzz about Mr. P at school was in a quiet cycle; kids who mentioned him mostly talked about whether or not their parents were going to go to the meeting my mother had told me about a couple of weeks ago. Actually I was so caught up in All-Stars practice that I hardly thought about Mr. P's being gay. Mostly I hoped that my mother hadn't been shooting off her mouth to other parents about seeing Mr. P at Macy's. I don't think she had, because no one at school said anything to me about it.

"I'm definitely going," Stacy Milstein's mom said. "I don't think gays should be in the schools, and I want to know what we can do to get him out."

"*If* he's gay," Ron's stepfather replied.

"Even if he is, so what?" said Mrs. Johansen, who seemed a lot more interested in discussing Mr. P than in taking Holly and Lee home. Holly beamed to hear her mother defend Mr. P. "He's the best teacher Holly's ever had, and that's all I care about. His private life is none of our business."

"It's our business if he's in contact with our kids," Mrs. Milstein said.

"Oh, come on," Mrs. Johansen said. "If the guy were married, he could be the biggest loser in the world, and it would never be an issue."

"It would be if he affected our kids," Mrs. Milstein said.

"Really?" Mrs. Johansen said. "Has your daughter

ever complained about having a mean teacher, or a teacher who favored some kids over others?"

A couple of parents smiled. Mrs. Milstein thought for a moment and said, "Well, her fourth-grade teacher was kind of a dud, but it wasn't anything she couldn't handle."

Ron's stepfather, Mr. Forman, said, almost to himself, "And then there's Pavlichek."

Three other adults nodded their heads. "Oh, God," one of them said.

"Math teacher," Mr. Forman explained to Holly's mom. "Absolutely ancient. Finally retired last year."

"Old witch," one of the other parents muttered.

"She hated boys, and according to Ron, she wasn't crazy about girls, either."

"Wait a minute," said Heather Rubin's mom unbelievingly. "Old Lady Pavlichek just retired last year?" Several parents nodded, and she shook her head. "God, *I* had her for math, what, twenty-five years ago. I thought she was old *then*. She really made me hate math."

Holly's mother made a gesture like *see what I mean?* "So she was a lousy teacher for years and years, but obviously nobody tried very hard to get rid of her. And I bet no one gave a damn about *her* personal life."

I was completely blown away by Mrs. Johansen's logic. No wonder Holly was a genius! Her mother was brilliant! And Mrs. Johansen didn't act like she was trying to make everybody else look stupid, either. She was really winning them over.

"Personally, I'd be just as happy if Padovano *were* gay," Heather's mom said. "At least I'd know Heather's not in any danger from him. She's so lovely"—a couple of parents gave her a gimme-a-break look, and Holly pretended to gag—"and he's very good-looking. Heather told me half the girls have had a crush on him."

"But if he is gay, doesn't that put the boys at risk?" Ron's stepfather asked.

"Does Ron have Mr. Padovano for social studies now?" Holly's mom asked.

"No, last year."

"Was there ever any of this talk about him last year?"

"No, I don't think so," Mr. Forman said. "Hey, Ron, come here." Ron and a few other kids went over to the parents. "When did the rumors about Mr. Padovano's being gay get started?"

"I don't know," Ron said. "I think the end of seventh grade, I started to hear guys talk about him, like they'd say 'that faggot.'"

"Kids are always doing that," one of the dads said dismissively.

"Well, they sounded like they meant it. But they were these stupid greaser types who were pissed off because Mr. P actually wanted to teach them something," Ron added quickly. "I never took it seriously."

"How long has Padovano been teaching in West River?" Mr. Forman asked.

"Five years," one of the moms said. "My David's a senior now; he had Padovano for eighth, and that was Padovano's first year at the junior high."

"And you never heard any rumors about his being gay?"

"Nothing," she said firmly.

The other parents all looked thoughtful, and just then my mom came in, shaking out her umbrella. Please, God, please, make her keep her mouth shut. Let her have temporary laryngitis. Not a sore throat, just so she can't talk.

"Seems to me I've only been hearing about this in the past few months," another dad said.

"That's right," said Holly, who was standing next to her mom. "The only reason anybody's been talking about Mr. P at all is because about three months ago some malicious *penis* wrote *FAGGOT* in big letters on Mr. P's car."

A few parents smiled at Holly's choice of words. "That's quite an image, Hol," Mrs. Johansen said, sounding embarrassed and amused at the same time.

"Well, you know what I mean. The whole thing stinks," Holly said.

"That's what started all the rumors?" Ron's stepfather asked.

"So there's no reason to think the guy's actually gay," another dad said.

"Oh, he's gay," my mother said. No, please no.

"How do you know?" Mrs. Johansen challenged.

"Janice and I saw him at Macy's a couple of weeks ago, with his, you know, his friend. His *boyfriend*," Mom said meaningfully.

"Janice, is that true?" Mrs. Milstein asked.

"I wouldn't want to jump to any conclusions," I said uncomfortably. No way was I going to stand there and say, yeah, Mr. P was with his boyfriend.

"Oh, Janice, you know it's true," Mom said. "Just

the way they looked at each other, you could tell they had a thing going." I held my breath, waiting for her to add, "In fact, they're living together," but she didn't, so she must not have heard them talking, thank goodness.

The group of parents were stunned. Holly glared at me like she wanted to set me on fire: *You knew all this time and didn't tell me?*

"Are you going to the meeting at the legion hall?" Mrs. Milstein asked.

"Yeah, I want to hear what people have to say," Mom said.

"That meeting sounds like a witch-hunt," David's mother said.

"If that's true, I think we should have a group of parents there in support of Mr. Padovano," Mrs. Johansen said.

"Count me in," David's mom said.

"Me too," Ron Kempner's stepfather said.

Some of the parents looked at him, surprised. "I thought you felt he might be a risk for the boys," Mrs. Milstein said.

Mr. Forman shook his head. "Think about it. I presume the man's been gay, if he *is* gay, the entire time he's been teaching here, yet it's only now that we're aware of it. If he were a threat to our kids, we'd have heard something a long time ago." Ron smiled proudly at his stepfather as several parents nodded.

"The bottom line is, Mrs. Johansen's right. The man's private life is none of our business," David's mother said.

"Well, I still don't like it," Mrs. Milstein said. "You

see these militants on TV—they act like they won't be happy until everybody's gay."

"That's ridiculous," David's mom said. "Just because they look strange doesn't mean they're recruiting, and anyway, Padovano certainly isn't like that."

"He might get that way," my mother said. Oh, Mom, please, be ignorant somewhere else!

"It can't hurt to go to a meeting," Mrs. Milstein said stubbornly.

A bunch of parents huddled around Holly's mom and began to trade phone numbers as Mom yanked me out of the bowling alley. It was clear that a lot of the parents standing there supported Mr. P or at least weren't threatened by him, but the danger caused by Mom's big mouth was done. Sunday night our phone didn't stop ringing: A zillion people wanted to know the dirt on Mr. P. And all day Monday I was bombarded with questions: What does his boyfriend look like? What was he wearing? How did they act like boyfriends? What did they say to you and your mom? Where do they live? Even in period six, right in front of Mr. P! Where in Macy's? Did Mr. P introduce the guy as his boyfriend? Did they kiss each other? By practice time I couldn't look Mr. P in the eye. Meanwhile, Holly was still mad at me for keeping Mr. P's friend a secret from her for two weeks.

Having kept quiet about Kevin's painting the car for three months, I found it pretty easy not to answer anybody's questions about Mr. P and his friend. "I'd rather not say," I kept telling people. "It's none of our business." But the rumors started getting wilder: Mr. P had demonstrated in front of St. Patrick's Cathedral. Mr. P

112

was infected with AIDS. Mr. P had put his hand on a boy's shoulder in period three and the kid had screamed, "Don't touch me, faggot," and punched him. Mr. P and his boyfriend brought high school guys to their apartment. Mr. P's period-one class told him they didn't want a homo teaching them and walked out.

I realized that Mr. P was acting different lately. He used to touch kids a lot, totally innocent stuff: pats on the shoulder, high fives. Now he was strictly hands-off. Before, he was always all over the room all period, but now he stayed behind his desk and at the front of the room most of the time. He kept to himself; you never saw him walking around at lunchtime anymore. It was a lot harder for him to get our class settled down every day, and sometimes he acted as if he didn't even care if we were too noisy.

By Tuesday things were getting ugly. Someone painted his car again, thank goodness in tempera paint that washed right off, and the same creep (same paint) wrote *GET LOST QUEER* on his classroom door at lunchtime. It was still there period six, which is when the custodian came to wash it off. The principal, Mr. Covello, came with him and asked Mr. P to step into the hall.

"I bet he's gonna get fired," Patty Zymont said.

"You can't fire someone just for being gay," Holly said.

"Not true," Kevin said.

"How do you know?" Holly asked.

"I just do," he said.

"He's right," Felicia Rim said.

"How do *you* know?" Holly said.

"My uncle's a lawyer," Felicia said. "I asked him, and he said it depended on the school district's policy."

Heather poked Rachel Strauss, who sat closest to the half-open door. "See if you can hear anything."

We all got quiet and Rachel went as close to the doorway as she could without being seen. "I think Mr. Covello asked Mr. P if he wanted to take some time off, and Mr. P said now wasn't a good time with the All-Stars only a few days away," she whispered after listening for a few seconds. Holly beamed at me, the first time she'd been friendly in two days.

"What else?" Patty whispered.

"Mr. Covello said fine, but he'd understand if Mr. P wants to take a few days off after the competition," Rachel said.

"Squeeze play," one of the guys muttered.

"Padovano's dead meat, ha-ha-ha," Jimmy De Milio said.

The door opened a little wider and Rachel scrambled back to her seat. Mr. P came in and took up the lesson as if nothing had happened, but within hours it was fresh blood for the Rumor Patrol: Watch for Mr. P to get fired right after the All-Stars.

As soon as I sat down on the school bus Wednesday morning, I felt a wad of paper hit me on the neck. I spun around angrily, expecting to see Kevin grinning his "Gotcha!" grin, but he pointed unsmilingly at the floor. I picked up the paper he'd hit me with: not a wad, but what looked like a folded note. Opening it, I read, "If you think I was yesterday's artist, you're out of your tiny little mind." Turning around, I waved my hand from side to side and made a don't-worry-about-it face, then ripped the note into sixteen pieces and stuffed them in my coat pocket. Funny, that hadn't even occurred to me.

Holly came up to me in homeroom. "I'm sorry I got mad at you. My mom says you were right not to say anything, even to me."

"I wanted to tell you," I said. "It was awful, carrying around a secret like that and wondering when my mother was gonna blow it."

"I wouldn't have told anybody if you had told me," Holly said.

"Oh, I know, it's not that I didn't trust you," I said. "I just thought, something like this, it was important not to tell *anybody*. I mean, the only person who has a right to say anything is Mr. P."

"That's what my mom said." Holly gave me a hug as the bell rang. "I guess I can tell you anything, because you sure know how to keep a secret."

That felt good.

I couldn't convince Mom to let me ride home with Mr. P, and she kept picking me up every day, which was deeply embarrassing. A couple of days before the competition, she was late getting to school, and Mr. P wasn't driving Holly home because her dad was taking her shopping for a birthday present for her mom. I sat on one of the benches, wishing I'd worn a heavier coat.

Mr. P came out of the main entrance and saw me sitting there. "Everything okay?" he asked.

Oh, sure, everything's fine, I thought. My mother's an ignorant bigot, the school's trying to force you to quit, and part of West River Junior High's academic honor is riding on my shoulders this Saturday. "Yeah, my mom's just late," I said.

"Okay," he said. "See ya tomorrow."

"Wait," I said. "Can I talk to you for a second?"

"Sure," Mr. P said, sitting next to me.

My throat tightened up; I was so ashamed. "Mr. P, I feel really bad about everything that's been going on this week," I said. "My mother told a big group of people Sunday about seeing you and your friend at Macy's."

"Uh-*huh*," Mr. P said, as if that cleared up some question he'd had.

"I really wanted to kill her," I said. "I wouldn't have told anybody in a zillion years. Do you believe me?"

"Absolutely," Mr. P said. "Really, Jan, I do. I know you're not a blabbermouth."

I hesitated for a moment. "Mr. P, are you . . . in good health?"

He smiled a little. "If you're asking do I have the AIDS virus, no, I don't. Neither does Paul. We both feel very, very lucky for that, because we've lost a lot of friends to AIDS."

I let that sink in, trying to imagine what it would be like if a lot of my friends died. "Do your parents know you're gay?" I asked.

"I told them a few years ago," he said. "They're okay with it. They took it hard at first, but they came around. I think it helps that I have brothers and sisters producing grandchildren for them."

I was really curious about his relationship with Paul, but I didn't want to sound like the nosy creeps who'd been talking about him since Sunday. "Do you go to any gay-rights demonstrations?" I asked.

"No, not really," he said. "Paul goes sometimes. To be perfectly honest, demonstrations are a little too public for me."

"It makes me so mad, the way people are acting. I want to go around punching people out. Especially my mother!"

"It's been painful," Mr. P agreed. "But don't blame your mom. If you and she hadn't seen us, somebody else from school probably would have."

"Why don't you just tell everybody to go to hell?" I burst out. "Tell them you're gay, and it doesn't make any difference, you're not gonna make anybody sick or try to convert anybody, and why don't they just forget it?"

"It doesn't work that way," he said. "For one thing, I could lose my job."

"Then Felicia was right," I said.

"About what?"

"When you were talking to the principal yesterday, Kevin said you could be fired just for being gay and Felicia said he was right. Her uncle's a lawyer and he said so. Do you think they'll fire you?"

"Right this minute, they'd have a hard time. I have tenure, and they have no cause to fire me. If I came out as gay, they might interpret that as cause. More likely, they'd try to make me miserable enough to quit. Of course, they could do that even if I didn't come out."

I could feel my whole face falling down into sad lines. I didn't even want to think about what school would be like without Mr. P. "You know there's a bunch of parents organizing this meeting next week."

"Yeah, I heard about it," Mr. P said. "Whatever happens there, I'll have to deal with it."

I couldn't believe how calm he was. "They're all out to get you!" I cried, close to tears. "Aren't you mad?"

Mr. P sighed. "Sure, I'm angry," he said. "It's frustrating to know that I'm a good teacher who cares about his students, in a decently paying job, in a school where the students are motivated to learn if only because their parents push them so damn hard, and it all may be jeopardized because people can't accept something about me that's as basic as . . ." He searched for a comparison.

"As having brown hair or wearing sweaters," I said.

He looked at me in a way Holly had once or twice, a look that said, *You understand.* "That's right, Jan," he said.

I saw my mother's tanklike station wagon turn off the road. "There's my mom," I said.

"Don't worry about me, Janice," Mr. P said, getting up. "You concentrate on Saturday."

"Yes, sir," I said, saluting. "See ya tomorrow."

118

❧ 13 ❧

"Scarsdale, Tuttle—where the heck is Tuttle Intermediate?"

The woman getting all the junior highs in line to enter the All-Stars assembly screamed at an assistant to find Tuttle Intermediate School's team *now* as Mr. P arranged us in size order. Karen Levant, who's a munchkin, was first, carrying the flag with *WEST RIVER* printed on it and acting as if it weighed half a ton. Mr. P, as coach, was next, then Holly, Shawn Choi, Ron, me, Kevin, and finally Sheila, who is far and away the tallest girl at West River Junior High. She has short, bristly hair and is so skinny that she looks like the world's largest bottle brush.

"Touch me, even by accident, and you're dead," I said to Kevin.

He made a face. "Don't worry, Green, if I wanted to molest animals I'll go to the zoo."

"Yeah, I hear your cousin the elephant is saving some hay for you," I sneered. Sheila giggled and Kevin

119

started to come back with a fresh insult, but Mr. P called back, "Janice, Kevin, cut it out."

"Yes, Dennis," Kevin fluted quietly. I glared at him and he looked away.

We looked around at the other schools, comparing team outfits: sixty different blazers, sweatshirts, jackets, T-shirts, sweaters, and caps in at least twenty different colors. We had really nice blue satin baseball jackets with *WEST RIVER* stitched in white across the backs. The only thing I didn't like was that I had to take an extralarge, same size as Kevin. Sheila took a medium, but the sleeves only went about halfway down her arms.

The Academic All-Stars competition was over except for the assembly. We'd spent the morning taking the tests in this huge high school in Westchester. They were all pretty hard, though I thought I got all the Super Quiz questions about *Pudd'nhead Wilson* right. Then we had this terrible lunch in the school cafeteria, which was about the size of a football field, where Kevin amused himself by throwing raisins one by one on the floor and watching people squish them and get them stuck to their shoes.

From inside the auditorium we heard the high school's band strike up the theme from "Masterpiece Theatre." It had played four times by the time we got to the back of the auditorium. "Hold the flag up, Karen," Mr. P said for the tenth time, and we filed in.

The back of the hall where the parents sat was bristling with Nikons and Canons and video cameras; my dad had his up and running the second he saw the

West River pennant. "Janice! Over here!" my mother screamed.

We got into our row behind Washington. The last three teams came in and the band finished the "Masterpiece Theatre" theme with a big flourish. Then the local superintendent of schools welcomed everyone to the All-Stars assembly and immediately killed the excitement by introducing a bunch of state and local school officials, who all made incredibly boring speeches.

Finally it was time for the teams to go up and get their trophies. When we stood up for our turn, there was this little rush down the far aisle: my dad with his video camera, Shawn's dad with his, Ron's stepfather clicking away with a self-winding Nikon like he was at some movie star's wedding, and another dad I didn't know with a camera. They were all positioned to shoot us coming off the stage, and when Ron and Shawn and I compared notes later, we found out that Kevin had behaved himself on stage, but all our dads had photographed him coming off the stage making a dog face, with his tongue hanging out.

Yorktown Heights sat down with their trophies, and it was time for the last and most suspenseful part of the program: the announcement of who won the Super Quiz. We had taken it first thing in the morning, so the competition officials had had time to feed all the little computer sheets through the grader and figure out which teams did best.

"And now, the moment we've all been waiting for . . . though if you like, we can just announce the Super Quiz winners in the mail with the results of the rest of the competition," the All-Stars coordinator said.

"Noooooooooo!" we all chorused.

"Okay, then, here we go." I began to feel a little sick to my stomach. Mr. P had warned us not to get our hopes up about the Super Quiz, since we had sixty other schools to beat, but most of us thought we did pretty well.

"And now, the winners," the coordinator said. "In third place, Bronxville Middle School!"

Across the auditorium, the team from Bronxville jumped out of their seats and started yelling, shoving their fists in the air as the rest of us applauded. The coordinator smiled at them until they settled down. "In second place," she said, "West River Junior High School!"

No way! We placed! "*AAAAAAAAAA!*" I screamed. "YES!" Mr. P yelled. We all jumped up and started hugging one another. Mr. P hugged Holly, Holly hugged Shawn, Ron hugged me, and I hugged Sheila, while we all screamed in one another's ears and our parents whipped out the cameras. Kevin was too macho to hug anybody, but he let out an "Awright!" and slapped Sheila and me on the back, almost sending Sheila flying into the next row.

Mount Kisco and New Rochelle tied for first place, and suddenly the coordinator was thanking us for coming, and it was all over.

"What now?" Ron asked.

"Now we're supposed to wait our turn for an official team photo, but we're so far back, it'll take at least forty-five minutes," Mr. P said. Several of us made a face. "Listen, we can sneak out the back," Mr. P said. "I got some good shots of you before, and we'll get

Ron's folks to take a few more. Find your parents and we'll meet at the tree where we took pictures earlier."

He led us out a side door near the stage and around the auditorium to the front lawn, where all the parents were milling around. I went over to my parents with Holly, and Kim started jumping up and down screaming. "You won! You won!"

"Just second," I said.

"That's good, considering how many teams there were," Mom said. She looked really proud. "Congratulations, you two."

"Mom, Mr. P wants us to get together for a team photo," I said, waving them over to where we were supposed to meet.

"Okay, but just for a minute; we have to get home," Mom said.

We went over to the rest of the team. Mr. P got us into position for a photo, but Kevin wasn't there. "Where is he?" Mr. P asked.

Sheila, who could see over everybody's heads, pointed and said, "He's going off with his family, over there."

"His folks came?" I said, surprised.

"Janice, run and get him," Mr. P said. "I want us all together."

"Why me?" I whined.

"Just go—hurry up," he said.

I ran in the direction Sheila had pointed and caught up with Kevin. He was with his parents—the other father with the camera turned out to be his dad, a big blond guy who looked a lot like Kevin—and another man, a friendly-looking guy who looked younger than Mr. P but who moved like an old man, leaning on a cane. "Hi, Mrs. Lynch. Kevin, Mr. P wants all of us for pictures," I said breathlessly.

"He took pictures before the assembly," Kevin said.

"Yeah, but now the parents can take pictures of us with him in them."

"Oh, right, that's the one I'm gonna put in a silver frame next to my bed," Kevin said. "Forget it, Green, it's over. I've got a life to live."

"Oh, come on, Kev, you put this much time into it, you can spare another couple of minutes," the man with the cane said.

"All right," Kevin said, not too thrilled about it.

We started back to the team. "Are you Kevin's brother?" I asked.

A smile brightened his thin face. "Yeah, how'd you know?"

"Just a guess. He told me and my friend Holly a lot about you, how he likes visiting you in the city. I wish I had a brother who lived in the Village."

"Yeah, well, he hasn't been down since January, he's been so busy cramming for this All-Stars thing. Calls me on the phone a lot, though. It's all he talks about. Amazing how much math I've forgotten since junior high." Kevin gave his brother an annoyed look. "I haven't seen him take anything so seriously since his first Communion. Remember that, Mom?" he said to Kevin's mother. " 'Who made you?' 'God made me,' " he said in a little-boy voice. That was too much for Kevin, who started walking faster to separate himself from his family.

"It's really nice of you to come up here just for the assembly," I said.

"Couldn't miss Kevin's moment of triumph," he said. "Plus I wanted to meet this Padovano guy. Kev never stops talking about him either."

"He's already got a boyfriend," Kevin's father muttered, just loud enough to hear.

Kevin turned around and yelled, "Hey, Green, come on and move it!" I gave his brother a little wave and ran ahead, thinking about what Mr. Lynch had said. Kevin's brother was gay, and he kind of looked like he wasn't . . . in good health.

All the parents with cameras took pictures of the team with Mr. P, then Ron's stepfather took a few with Mr. P's camera. Kevin tried to get away fast, but his brother went up to Mr. P and introduced himself. Mr. P said hi and looked at him searchingly. "You look familiar," he said.

Kevin's brother shrugged. "Ever get down to the Village?"

"Once in a blue moon," Mr. P said.

"I was probably that face across the room at some loft party," Kevin's brother said.

Kevin started to look scared. "We're outa here!" he bellowed. He practically dragged his family off to the parking lot.

Everybody else was going for pizza with Mr. P, but my mother shook her head before I could even ask. "Daddy and I have a dinner date in Jersey," she said.

"Can't I go with them?" I asked. "Ron's folks can take me home."

"Just come home with us, Janice," Mom snapped.

She and Kim asked a lot of questions about the competition, but I was too P.O.'d to say much. "You must be exhausted," Mom finally said.

"Yeah, I'm real tired." I was, too. Tired of having secrets to keep.

14

The principal announced our second-place Super Quiz finish on the P.A. system Monday morning, right after the Pledge of Allegiance, and Tuesday they hung a big CONGRATULATIONS banner over the main corridor, replacing the one with all our names on it that had been up for a couple of weeks. People I didn't even know said "Way to go!" and we were all interviewed for the school newspaper. But I didn't see anybody congratulate Mr. P, not even in period six.

The parents' meeting at the American Legion hall was scheduled for Thursday night at seven, and as it got close, it was all anyone could talk about. I begged Daddy to come home early and go with Mom, thinking he might understand how dumb the whole thing was. He said he was really sorry, but he had to work late. The rumors kept flying: Mr. P kept staring at this boy in his period-three class; Mr. P was getting fired on Friday; the parents were going to find out where Mr. P lives and demonstrate in front of his house. I kept saying, "That's stupid, that's stupid, that's stupid," till I felt like a robot—but, unlike a robot, I got more and more scared every hour.

"I don't see why we can't come with you," I said to Mom.

"Yeah," Kim said.

"It's not a place for children," she said. "God knows what kinds of things people are going to talk about."

"Mom, they aren't gonna talk about anything I haven't heard about on TV or read about in the paper."

"Well, there are things I don't particularly want Kim to hear," Mom said.

"Mom, get real; Kim watches 'Donahue' every single day," I said exasperatedly. "She probably knows more about gay people than you and me put together."

"Yeah," Kim said. Mom gave her a don't-*you*-start look. "I wanna go."

"You're not going, either one of you, and that's all there is to it," Mom said, putting on her coat. "Kim, upstairs at nine, and no TV if your homework isn't done. Janice, I'm counting on you."

"Yeah, sure," I said sullenly. The second I heard the garage door close I ran to the phone. "You really wanna go to this meeting?" I asked Kim, punching Holly's number.

"Sure," Kim said excitedly.

" 'Cause I can't leave you home," I said, listening to the rings. Please still be home, please, please.

Holly picked up. "Johansen residence," she said.

"Hol, it's me. Can we come to the meeting with you?"

From Holly's end I heard her mother call, "Who is it?" Holly yelled to her, "It's Janice; she wants to come with us."

"Let me talk to her," Mrs. Johansen said, her voice getting closer. Then into the phone she said, "Hi, Janice?"

"Mrs. J, can you bring Kim and me to the meeting? My mom totally refused to take us."

"Honey, if your mom doesn't want you there, I don't think it's right for me to take you."

"But I've got to be there!" I pleaded. "You said yourself it was important for everyone who supported Mr. P to be there!"

"I meant adults, Janice."

"Aren't you taking Holly? Isn't Ron going?"

"Well, yes, but . . . Janice, I just can't. I know you love Mr. P, but if I bring you and Kim, your mother'll kill you first and then come after me."

I was desperate. "If you don't take us, I'll just call a taxi."

She hesitated, then sighed. "All right. I'll be there in fifteen minutes."

"Thank you, thank you," I said. I scribbled a note for the refrigerator door so Mom wouldn't get totally hysterical.

By the time we got there at a quarter to eight, the legion hall was packed. Mom was sitting next to Mrs. Milstein on the far side of the room. The "pro-Padovano" people were sitting and standing in the back of the hall. Mrs. Johansen and Mr. Forman must have been hitting the phones big time, because there were a lot of them, including several teachers and the rabbi from our temple. Our principal, Mr. Covello, was sitting on the platform up front, the light gleaming off his big, bald head, along with a few people I guessed were leaders of the group that wanted to get rid of Mr. P. I didn't want my mother to see Kim or me, so we melted into the crowd in the back and tried to become invisible.

"Hi, Linda," Mr. Forman said to Mrs. Johansen. "We were getting worried."

"Yeah, sorry," Mrs. Johansen said. "What's it been like so far?"

"People making speeches about the evils and dangers of homosexuality. The one speaking now is typical." A redheaded woman standing on the platform was talking about how gays and lesbians were trying to push into every aspect of American life and get a lot of attention from the media even though they know perfectly well that almost everybody thinks homosexuality is unnatural and disgusting.

"Charming," Mrs. Johansen said after listening for a moment.

"They started pretty much on time, with one of those generic prayers," Mr. Forman said. "Something along the lines of, 'Heavenly Father, guide us in bringing our efforts to fruition.'" Very nice, I thought. *Dear God, help us get this teacher fired.* "Then they said the Pledge of Allegiance, and then the speeches started. The woman talking now is the last one on the platform except for the principal."

"Has anyone talked specifically about Mr. Padovano?"

"Well, not by name," Mr. Forman said. "The first woman who spoke said we were gathered because of concerns over the presence of a gay teacher on the West River Junior High faculty, so it was pretty clear whom she meant. Oh, and they're passing around a petition demanding that the school district investigate the sexual preference of job candidates and dismiss anyone currently on the staff who is discovered to be gay."

"I'm sure that's illegal, at least the first part," Mrs. Johansen said. "Any complaints about Padovano other than his being gay?"

"No, but the night is young," Mr. Forman said.

The redheaded woman finished speaking (to applause from most of the audience) and sat down as another woman got up. "Thank you, Mrs. Leahy," she said. "Now I'd like to introduce the principal of West River Junior High, Mr. Covello, who will make a short statement and answer any questions you have."

Mr. Covello got up, mopping his sweaty bald head. The other people on the platform looked all fired up, but he just looked uncomfortable. "Thank you, Mrs. Grainger." Aha, so that was Cory's mom. "Parents, as a representative of the junior high administration, I want you to know that we take your concerns very seriously."

"Does that mean you're gonna fire the gay teacher?" a parent called out.

"At this time, we have no cause to dismiss the teacher in question," Mr. Covello said. "He is on the permanent faculty, that is to say he has tenure; evaluations of his work have been excellent; and he has not declared his sexual orientation to us, nor is he required to."

"Oh, come on, everybody knows he's a homo," a man boomed out.

"Says who, a bunch of kids?" a voice called from the back of the room.

"A kid's *mother* saw him and his boyfriend in a store, holding hands," someone else yelled out.

"Who?" several people called out. "Is she here?" "Where is she?"

I went cold all over, thinking that Mom was going to jump up and say, *Here I am, I saw them*, the way she did at the bowling alley. But to my surprise, Mom stayed in her seat, and Mrs. Milstein started whispering to her but didn't point her out to the group. The other parents who had been at the bowling alley didn't point her out either.

"Why doesn't Mom raise her hand?" Kim whispered.

"Shut up," I said. "It's better if she doesn't."

"The kid's name is Janice Green," said a woman I recognized as Jimmy De Milio's mother.

"That's right, the mother is Carol Green," Mrs. Grainger said. "I spoke to her on the phone last week. Mrs. Green, are you here?"

A hundred heads were craning around, looking for Mom, who still didn't move. I was starting to hope they'd decide she wasn't there when a woman sitting in front of her said, "Excuse me, aren't you Mrs. Green? I remember you from Woodbine Elementary. Our girls were in the same sixth grade." Before Mom could even answer, the woman yelled, "She's right here!"

People called out for her to tell what she'd seen, and a woman behind her actually started to poke at her shoulder to get her to stand up. Finally Mom got up. She said, "I'd rather not talk about what I saw" and sat down.

The folks in the back of the hall looked kind of pleased, but the others weren't about to let her off the hook. "Tell us!" "We want to know!" they yelled. After a moment Mr. Covello gestured for quiet. "Mrs. Green, it would really be helpful if you told us what you witnessed that day. I think some firsthand knowledge would settle some of the rumors flying around."

Mom stood up slowly, looking almost sick. What was the big deal? You're one of the people who got Mr. P in trouble, Mom, so just narc on him and sit down; you're among friends. Then I looked around and realized she *wasn't* among friends. She hardly knew anybody there except the people from temple, and most of them thought she was being a major fink. Most of her friends—the women she'd grown up with, her college friends—live outside West River. And I couldn't remember a time she'd ever spoken in front of a group. Jeez, I thought, Mom's *shy*.

By the time she spoke, the room was dead quiet. "My daughter and I were in Macy's last month, and we ran into Mr. Padovano in the men's department," she said in a flat voice. "He was with another man. They were holding up sweaters to see how they looked on each other. Other than that, they didn't touch. Mr. Padovano saw my daughter, and he came over to where we were and introduced us to his friend. That's what he called him, his friend."

"Did you hear them say anything to each other?" Mrs. Grainger asked.

"No, I didn't," Mom said.

"That's not the way you told it earlier," a dad said impatiently. "My son's friend told him that you told a group of parents that Padovano was definitely gay, that you could tell from the way they looked at each other."

"I did say that, and it did look that way to me," Mom said. "But I could be mistaken. That's all I have to say." And she sat down.

❧ 15 ❧

*E*verybody broke into excited murmurs. "I still think he's a homo," said the man with the booming voice. "Regular guys don't stand in a store and try sweaters on each other."

"Oh, shut up, Ingram," another dad said. "You think anyone's queer who doesn't drink a six-pack and slap his wife around every night."

Mr. Ingram, who looked like a major bully, jumped up. "Look, Cooper, I'll punch your lights out," he yelled.

He started for the other dad, and it took four people to pull him back. People were hollering "Sit down!" and "Take it outside!" Mr. Covello and Mrs. Grainger were yelling for quiet, but nobody listened until some dad stuck his fingers in his mouth and let out a piercing whistle.

"Folks, settle down, please," Mr. Covello said, mopping his head again. "I'm happy to take more questions, but we're all going to have to stay calm."

A mother raised her hand and was recognized by Mr. Covello. "I'm here not just because Mr. Padovano is gay, but because he's a bad influence on our children in other ways," she said. "He told my Betsy's class that religion was responsible for most of the suffering in the world."

The room buzzed again. "When did he say that?" another parent asked.

"It was last fall, when they were studying Latin America," the first mother said. "He said that the Spanish explorers used the bringing of Christianity as an excuse to enslave the natives and take their gold."

"That's exactly what they did do!" a parent called from the back.

"I don't want my son told that religion is responsible for crimes against thousands of people!" a woman cried.

"Then don't send your kid to a public school, lady!" yelled the guy who had supported the statement about the conquistadors.

"I pay taxes for the public schools!" the woman said.

"People, please," Mr. Covello said. "Let's not get into philosophical arguments. Please confine yourself to discussion of the teacher in question."

"Fine," another woman called out. "Ever since my kid's had Padovano as a teacher, all she does is argue with me. She doesn't like the way we throw out the garbage or the way I talk about the cleaning woman or what we spend our money on or what her father and I do for a living. She questions everything we do or say!"

"How are kids gonna learn if they don't ask questions?" Mr. Forman asked.

"She doesn't ask me questions, she challenges me!" the woman yelled. "She acts like everything I think is wrong! I don't need it!"

"My kid's the same way; he's driving me nuts!" a dad said.

"Padovano assigns these special projects that take hours of research, and they always seem to involve the rest of the family," another parent said. "I wind up spending almost as much time on them as he does!"

"All I've heard at home for almost two solid years is Mr. P says this, Mr. P says that!"

"I hear he can't control his classes!"

Mrs. Johansen had had her hand in the air for a while, and now she started waving it a little more aggressively to get Mr. Covello's attention. He finally pointed at her and said, "Yes, this lady down here."

She came right to the front of the crowd, though not onto the platform. "My name is Linda Johansen, and my family and I just moved to West River in November," she said. "One of the reasons we moved to this community was that we'd heard the schools were first-rate. They *are* good, but part of why they're good is teachers like Dennis Padovano.

"My daughter, Holly, is very bright—I'm sorry, honey, I have to tell them," she said as Holly turned eight shades of crimson. "She was bored to death in the schools she attended upstate. Mr. Padovano is probably the first teacher ever to challenge her intellectually. And I have to tell you, I think those special projects are wonderful. I've learned as much as Holly has. In a way, I'm glad we got away from the gay issue, which is meaningless until and unless Mr. Padovano

137

himself says anything about it, and we're discussing his merits as a teacher. I'm glad that Holly questions the world around her and even that she challenges my opinions and beliefs. It's a pain in the neck sometimes, but I'd rather have a child who challenges what she thinks is wrong than a child who's going to let the world push her around."

"I still don't want a degenerate teaching my children," the redheaded woman on the platform said.

Mrs. Johansen's face went blank for a second, and I could tell she was trying not to look angry. But instead of yelling, "He's not a degenerate!" (which is what I would have done), she smiled at the woman.

"Even though we disagree on this issue, I want you to know that I respect your point of view and understand your concerns," Mrs. Johansen said, sounding totally convincing. She gestured to the people on the platform and the people sitting in the rows in front of her. "You're right to be very, very protective about who teaches our children, just as I am. That's why I decided to find out as much as I could about this issue before coming here tonight—do my homework, so to speak." A few people chuckled.

"I did some research in the library, and I also called a friend of mine who works in the New York City schools. In fact, last year she started teaching in the city's special high school for gay teenagers. She said she went in there with a whole lot of assumptions about gay men and lesbians—all of them wrong, she told me—and she's learned a lot. She helped me summarize the points I want to make to you tonight.

"Based on reported incidents, it's very, very rare for

a gay teacher to take advantage of a student sexually, much more rare than for a heterosexual teacher to misbehave with a student of the opposite sex. My friend said that every gay teacher she knows takes special care *never* to become physically involved with a student, even when approached by the student. Second, and I know many of you know this already, the evidence points increasingly to homosexuality as being something that's present in people from birth, not something you can choose to be or learn to be.

"When you think about it, that means our fear of some gay teacher trying to recruit our children is really unfounded. According to my friend, her students didn't need anyone to tell them they were gay, and none of them became gay because someone they looked up to was gay. The bottom line for me is that no one can make our kids be anything they're not, and I don't want our community to lose one of its best teachers because people are afraid of something that's extremely unlikely to happen." Mrs. Johansen took a deep breath and smiled again. "Thanks for hearing me out. Oh, I've got copies of some of the articles I found if you're interested."

She stepped off the platform as about half the crowd applauded, including a few people in the front of the room. Mr. Covello stood up again and said, "Thank you, Mrs. Johansen, that was very edifying. Parents, I want to assure you again that the school district takes your concerns very seriously, and we are more than willing to listen to opinions on all sides of the matter we've discussed tonight."

Mrs. Grainger leaned forward and asked, "Mr.

Covello, what's your feeling, personally, about working with a gay teacher?"

Mr. Covello half turned and looked at her without expression. "I don't think that's relevant," he said. "My job is to see that our students are educated as we are directed by the State Board of Regents, and it would be inappropriate for my personal feelings to affect that process."

Standing up, Mrs. Grainger said, "I don't think we're going to accomplish anything else here tonight." She and her friends stepped off the platform and headed for the door, stopping to collect the petition that had been circulating around the room. Several people ran after her and crossed off their names.

The platform people's departure sort of broke up the meeting. A lot of people followed them out, but they looked as if they'd had some of the wind taken out of their sails. A group gathered around Mr. Forman, and they started making plans for a petition in support of Mr. P. While Holly and Mrs. Johansen were handing out articles and talking to ten people at once, I stared at them, wondering what it would be like to be beautiful and a genius and have a beautiful genius mother you could always count on to stand up for what was right.

Kim pulled at me just in time to duck down again as my mother and Mrs. Milstein got up to leave. I peeked at her from the side of the bar at the back of the legion hall. A few people asked her questions, but she acted as if she didn't want to talk anymore. As she was leaving, I got a good look at her face. It had an expression on it I had never seen before. She looked totally confused.

16

Once Mom had left, my worry over the trouble I'd be in if she found me there shifted to total panic about the trouble I was going to be in when we got home. "I don't suppose there's any chance we could beat Mom home," I said to Mrs. Johansen.

" 'Fraid not," she said. "I'm willing to stay as long as people want to talk. That's the problem with going out on a limb, Janice—it tends to get lopped off." I must have looked as panicky as I felt, because she said, "Tell you what. I'll come in with you. Maybe a little adult backup will help."

"I hope," I said mournfully.

"Am I gonna get in trouble too?" Kim asked.

"Nah, you were just along for the ride." I looked at her, curious. "What did you think?"

"I think those people who want to fire Mr. P are stupid," Kim said. "What are they so upset about, anyway?"

"They think Mr. P's a bad influence because he's gay."

"What's wrong with it?" Kim asked.

141

"Nothing, as far as I'm concerned," I said. "But a lot of people think it's wrong, like it's not normal. Mom thinks it's wrong."

"Why? What do men do when they fall in love?"

"You mean how do they show it?"

"Yeah."

"Well, you know, hugging and kissing, just like men and women do."

"Don't they have sex?"

Oh, boy. Now I knew how Mom felt the first time I asked her about sex, not that she told me. "Yeah, but I'm not sure what," I said.

"Does Mom know?"

"Probably, but I don't think she's real eager to tell you," I said. "Listen, I'll look it up in a book, and if I find out, I'll tell you."

"Okay," Kim said. "You know, Jan, we can tell Mom it was my idea to come here. Maybe she won't get so mad."

"Thanks, Kim. I don't think Mom'll buy it, but it's a nice idea," I said gratefully. Suddenly Kim seemed more like a real person instead of Mom's little windup toy.

Mom had been gone from the meeting for at least twenty minutes by the time we all piled into Mrs. Johansen's Volvo. My hands were shaking as I unlocked the front door.

Mom marched into the front hall, my note from the fridge in her hand. In the family room, the TV exploded with sitcom laughter. "I see I was talking to myself when I told you not to go to that meeting," she said.

"I had to be there, Mom," I said. "It was important."

"Not when I expressly told you to stay home and watch your sister. Instead you drag her miles from home, where God knows what could have happened."

"Mom, I wanted to go with Janice," Kim said. "She didn't make me."

"You go upstairs," Mom snapped at Kim. "It's way past your bedtime." It was a little before nine-thirty. If this meeting hadn't happened, Kim would have still been arguing with Mom about letting her watch TV.

Kim started to protest, but Mom gave her such a mean look that she shriveled up like a raisin and went upstairs without another word. "Mom, you could see how many kids there were at that meeting," I said. "Kids younger than Kim, even. I mean, those parents weren't afraid of what their children were gonna hear. Anyway, what'd they say that was so awful?"

"I don't care what other parents did," Mom said. "I'm not going to put up with your defiance and irresponsibility."

"I didn't do anything irresponsible," I said. "Kim and I didn't walk to the meeting. I left you a note, and we were with Mrs. Johansen the whole time."

"Oh, and that makes it all right?" Mom asked. "Linda, what were you thinking, taking them? Didn't it occur to you that I wanted them home?"

"Janice begged me to take them, Carol," Mrs. Johansen said. "It was very important to her. She really wanted to be there to support Mr. Padovano."

"So what?" Mom yelled. "All you had to do was tell her no!"

"I tried to," Mrs. Johansen said. I was scared that

she was going to tell Mom that I would have gone anyway, but unlike some mothers I know, Mrs. Johansen
isn't a fink. "Carol, to be honest, I thought Janice's reasons for wanting to go were at least as valid as your
reasons for wanting her not to."

"Well, of course, I'd expect that attitude from *you*,"
Mom said. "But I also expect a grown woman to be a
little more responsible than a fourteen-year-old!"

"My mother is not irresponsible!" Holly said.

"Come on, Carol, it's not like your girls were in any
danger," Mrs. Johansen said. "Everybody there was
pretty reasonable."

"Including the two nuts who started fighting?" Mom
said. "Another minute and there could have been a
riot! I'm sorry, a responsible parent doesn't expose her
children, or especially other people's children, to
potentially violent situations!"

"I really think you're overdramatizing," Mrs.
Johansen said.

"I suppose you think a responsible mother lets a
fifteen-year-old daughter run around with boys doing
God knows what while she takes writers to cocktail
parties in the city every night!" Mom yelled.

One party. I'd told Mom that Mrs. Johansen had
gone with one author to one cocktail party. "Mom,
stop it!" I said.

By now Mrs. Johansen was trying to hold onto her
temper, and Holly looked mad enough to kick a hole in
the wall. "You're out of line, Carol," Mrs. Johansen
said. "I take good care of my kids, and my kids take
good care of themselves. Why don't you talk to Janice
instead of lashing out?"

"Don't tell me how to raise my child!" Mom yelled. "That stuff about kids challenging their parents is a lot of baloney! When I was a kid, I did what I was told, and I expect my kids to do what they're told!"

"Even when it's wrong?" I asked angrily. "Even when it's cruel or stupid?"

Mom raised her hand to hit me, then caught herself, realizing she'd be smacking me in front of other people. When she spoke, her voice sounded like a million-volt current going through a hot wire. "I may not be able to control who teaches my children or what their textbooks say or what kind of people they associate with at school, but I can damn well control where they go and what they do in my home. You're grounded," she said to me. "You'll come straight home from school every day and stay here until it's time for school again unless I take you someplace. You are not to talk on the phone unless I hand it to you, and you are not to have any visitors unless I invite them. We'll see how quick you are to defy me the next time you think you're smarter than I am. And don't go crying to your grandmother this time, 'cause it won't do any good."

Holly and her mom stared at us, Holly looking horrified and Mrs. Johansen just looking sad and sorry. "We'd better get home, Hol," she said.

As Holly opened the front door, my dad came up from the basement in pajamas and bathrobe, a screwdriver in one hand and the lamp from Kim's night table in the other. "What's going on?" he asked.

145

❧ 17 ❧

The next day at school was awful. I tried to apologize to Holly, but she was so angry over the awful things Mom had said that it spilled over onto me, and I was too ashamed of my mother to argue with her. (Being Holly, she got over it by lunchtime and was all sympathy when I told her I was grounded.) Meanwhile, all the other kids who supported Mr. P were mad at me because of what Mom had said at the meeting, even though she had watered down the story a little. I wanted to put a huge sign on the main bulletin board:

JANICE GREEN IS NOT RESPONSIBLE FOR
THE STATEMENTS OF HER IGNORANT,
FINKY MOTHER.

That weekend was the longest I've ever spent. I couldn't go anywhere, and Mom wouldn't let me use the phone, and she was watching me like a hawk. She wouldn't even let me go to Friday night services at temple. I don't go to temple very often, but a lot of

146

kids and their parents were going because the rabbi had been at the parents' meeting and they wanted to see if she was going to talk about Mr. P. Sure enough, on Monday I found out she'd talked about the meeting in her sermon and said that if God made everybody, that includes gay people, and anybody from our temple trying to get rid of Mr. P wasn't acting very Jewish. Mr. Forman and some other parents brought a petition supporting Mr. P, and practically every adult there signed it. Some kids said the same petition was at a few of the local churches Sunday morning.

There were also petitions all over school during the next week. The students had one that said we don't care if someone who works at our school is gay or straight as long as he or she does a good job and doesn't mess with us sexually. The teachers had one that said the same thing in more formal language, not just at the junior high but at the high school and the elementaries too, and we heard that way more than half the teachers signed it. Practically everybody signed the junior high petition, and Patty Zymont said her brother told her the high school kids were organizing in support of Mr. P too.

Mrs. Johansen and Mr. Forman organized a letter-writing campaign among the parents, and by Wednesday I was helping pass out flyers at school:

TELL YOUR PARENTS TO WRITE TO THE SCHOOL BOARD AND SUPPORT MR. PADOVANO!

They should tell the board:
1) He's a great teacher.

2) He's not gay unless *he* says he is.
3) Even if he *is* gay, it's no big deal.
4) Prejudiced board members can be voted out!

Things stayed chilly at home. I didn't speak to Mom unless she asked me direct questions, to which I would give one-word answers as coldly as possible. My father had made it clear that he was on Mom's side about punishing me for taking Kim to the meeting, so it was a big surprise when he came into my room one night while I was propped up on my bed doing an English assignment.

"You busy with homework?" Daddy asked.

"Not very."

"What's new at school?"

"Nothing."

"Any new developments with Mr. Padovano?"

Like you care, I wanted to say, but I was in enough trouble. "Not really."

"Your mother says there's a flyer going around asking parents to write the school board. She heard about it from Mrs. Milstein."

"Yeah," I said.

"You got one?"

"In my notebook, on the desk. It's orange."

He got the flyer out of my loose-leaf and read it. "Can I have this?"

"I suppose," I said, looking at my English essay and trying not to seem bothered. "You and Mom planning to write a little hate mail?"

"I don't know what your mother's doing, but I thought I'd let them know I don't think the guy is doing you any harm."

I looked up, surprised. "Doesn't Mom have you convinced that Mr. P's a dangerous pervert? I thought that was the party line around here."

"Your mom's not convinced of anything right now, Jan. She's very confused." Daddy pointed at the bed. "Can I sit down?" I shrugged, and he sat at the foot of the bed. "Your mother doesn't know what to think about Mr. Padovano anymore, and I think she's a little ashamed. She told me getting up and talking to those people was one of the worst experiences she's ever had."

"Gee, that's terrible," I said sarcastically. "Forgive me if I don't burst out crying for her, but I think what's happening to Mr. P is a lot worse than being uncomfortable speaking in front of a group." He didn't have an answer to that. "What's her problem with Mr. P, anyway? I asked Bubbie a few weeks ago, and all she could come up with was that Mom's afraid of anything unusual."

"Well, yeah, that's true, in a way," Daddy said. "Your mother has this image of how things are supposed to be, and she tends to not like anything that doesn't fit that image. And when it's something that she thinks affects her, or her family, she gets threatened by it."

Boy, did he have Mom nailed. That explained everything from her taste in movies to her reaction when we'd see homeless people in the city. "Well, that explains why she can't stand me," I said. "I don't begin to fit her idea of what a daughter should be."

Daddy looked horrified. "That's not true, Jan. Your mother loves you."

"I know that," I said. "But sometimes she acts more like she owns me, like I'm her dog or something, and

I have to do what she says or she'll bop me on the nose with a newspaper. And to her, I'll always be a bad dog, making messes on the carpet, because she wants some elegant Irish wolfhound, and I'm just this big old sheepdog."

"Is that really how you think your mother feels about you?" Daddy asked.

"That's how she acts sometimes," I said. "And, Daddy, I can't take her being such a control freak anymore. If she had her way, she'd control what I wear, who my friends are, and what I think. She's gonna have to get over that." Daddy didn't say anything, but he made a face like maybe-you've-got-a-point. "I just don't understand her," I said. "Why does everything have to be her way?"

"Jan, slow down," Daddy said. "Try to see it from her side. I know that to you, your grandmother is this sweet old lady who would give you the moon if you asked for it, but she had your mother very much under her thumb all her life, and she's often made your mother feel as if she didn't measure up. Sound familiar?" I nodded. I'd heard it on enough TV shows: People are the kind of parents their parents were. "Add the fact that your mother's raising two kids in a world that seems to get more out of control every year, and maybe you can see why she wants to stay on top of what she thinks she *can* control."

All of a sudden my father's a psychologist. "When did you figure all this out?" I asked.

"I've been giving it a lot of thought lately," he said. "I also think this is a conversation we should have had a long time ago, and for that I'm sorry."

150

"That's okay, I understand," I said, letting everything Daddy had said sink in. "You know, what you say makes sense, but that doesn't make it right for Mom to persecute Mr. P or to be on my case all the time."

"Well, as I said before, I have the feeling she's rethinking her position on Mr. Padovano. I also think your being grounded would stop if you'd apologize for disobeying her."

"Uh-uh," I said emphatically. "I didn't do anything wrong going to that meeting. I was standing up for what was right. She can ground me for life if she wants to, but I won't apologize for doing the right thing."

"Well, that's between you and your mother," Daddy said, standing up and going to the door. "Thanks for the flyer."

I turned back to my homework, sort of wishing Daddy had said he'd get Mom to unground me. But I guess if you're gonna stand up for what's right, you have to fight your own battles.

On Tuesday of the third week after the All-Stars competition, the results came in, and by period six, Holly, Sheila, and I were frantic. Kevin, of course, acted like he couldn't care less.

"Before we start class, I have some very pleasant news," Mr. P said right after the bell rang.

"He's decided to wear pearls to the spring dance," Jason Baron whispered.

"Shut up, you moron," Holly hissed.

"As you know, West River's Academic All-Stars team placed second in the Hudson Division in the Super Quiz, and now the rest of the results are in," Mr. P said. "Sitting among you right now are not one, not two, not three, but four winners of medals in individual events."

The four of us on the team looked at one another incredulously. Even Kevin looked stunned. "We all placed?" I asked.

"Yup." Mr. P grinned. "In the Honors category, Holly, you got a first place in math and a third in social studies; Janice, you got a second in the essay; and Sheila, you placed second in science. And our Varsity man, Kevin, got a first-place medal in social studies. Let's give them a hand!"

The rest of the class started clapping while Holly and I traded high fives. Kevin sat back with this goofy look on his face, like *Me? I won first prize?* and Sheila, as usual, just looked embarrassed. "What about the others?" Holly asked.

"Shawn got a third in science," Mr. P said.

"Who won the regional championship?" I asked.

"Mount Kisco," Mr. P said. "But we placed first in Orchard County and third in the whole division, which is pretty darn good." He told us that as far as he knew, this was the best a West River team had ever done in the All-Stars. It was by far the coolest news I'd heard all year.

"How was school today?" Mom asked when I got home.

"Fine," I said, taking my books upstairs.

That was one secret I didn't have to keep for long. Mom gave me a really weird look when we sat down for supper the next night. "What's new with every-body?" Daddy asked.

"Nothing with me, but I think Janice has some news," Mom said.

"I do?" I asked innocently.

"Sheila Mikulsky's mother told me the All-Stars team did very well."

"Yeah, it did."

"She congratulated me on your medal, Janice."

"You won a prize? Neat!" Kim said.

"Whatcha win?" Daddy asked.

"I placed second in the essay in my category," I said.

"Why didn't you tell us yesterday?" Mom demanded.

"I didn't think you'd be interested," I said.

"Janice," Daddy said.

"That's so neat! Did Holly win anything?" Kim asked.

I told them the rest of the results, trying to sound as blasé as possible. "Really, it's no big deal," I said.

"Of course it is," Mom said. "Mrs. Mikulsky said there's going to be a reception for all the winning schools on Monday. Can parents come?"

"Why do you ask? I'm not going," I said. "I'm *grounded*, remember?"

"Janice, come on," Daddy said.

"Of course you're going," Mom said.

"No, you can't have it both ways," I said. "You said school and that's it. Now you're willing to have me go someplace else because it'll give you pleasure. Well, too bad." Mom looked totally outraged.

"Won't it give you pleasure too?" Daddy asked.

"I'm trying to make a point here, and if I have to sacrifice something to do that, I will."

"You're being spiteful," Mom said. "You're only hurting yourself, you know."

"Then why are *you* so bummed? Don't you get it, Mom? I'm not your little puppy dog. If you keep trying to control everything I do, you're gonna wind up as miserable as I am."

Mom looked into her chicken and mashed potatoes for a moment. "You were wrong to go to that meeting without my permission," she said.

"No, I was wrong to sneak out behind your back," I said. "I should have stood up to you beforehand and told you that if you wouldn't take me, I'd go with the Johansens. If I'd done that, the only thing you'd be punishing me for is disagreeing with you."

"I don't need lessons in ethics from a fourteen-year-old," Mom said.

"How long ago was that meeting?" Daddy asked quickly.

"Two weeks tomorrow," I said.

"Carol, I think two weeks is long enough to be grounded for one act of disobedience," he said. Mom looked as if she was definitely thinking about it. "Don't you think you've both made your point?"

Mom sighed. "I suppose so." Whew. I would've died if Mom had said, *Fine, let her stay home.*

The All-Stars awards were given out at the same high school where the competition had taken place. We trooped across the stage for our individual medals as our names were called—Holly calm and poised,

Sheila hunched over like she was about to be scolded, Shawn running up as if he were shot out of a cannon, Kevin clowning—and gathered up there to get two team trophies. Assorted moms and dads took pictures, several of which included Mr. P looking prouder than all the parents put together. (I found it easy to smile that afternoon because Holly had told me some truly bizarre news in homeroom: My mother had called her mother on Sunday and *apologized*, which was the next best thing to her apologizing to me.) By Wednesday there were photos of us all over the bulletin board in the main hall, and that Friday we were honored at the student elections kick-off assembly.

The following Monday, we had a substitute teacher in period six.

❧ 18 ❧

The sub's name was Ms. Sivack. I'd seen her around school before. She was large and middle-aged and didn't look like she'd put up with too much nonsense. The first question we all asked on entering the classroom was "Where's Mr. Padovano?"

"I'll answer that when the bell rings," she said fifteen times. When the bell finally rang, she just stood there until we got quiet.

"I'm going to say this once," Ms. Sivack said. "The substitute office called me Friday and asked me to come in for Mr. Padovano all this week. He has indeed left a week's worth of lesson plans. They are crystal clear, and I intend to follow them. I have no idea why he's absent, so don't ask me."

"It's AIDS," Jason Baron said.

"Shut *up*," said Patty Zymont.

"He's not sick," Holly said. "He wouldn't know on Friday that he's gonna be sick for a whole week."

"He could be having tests in a hospital," Rachel Strauss said.

"He'd wait till next week, when we're on vacation," Holly said.

"Not if it's urgent," Jason said, leering at us. "Not if he has AIDS."

"You're a nerfbrain, Baron," Kevin said. "An AIDS test takes five minutes."

"How do you know?" Jason asked him.

Kevin's face got pink. "Everybody knows that," he said. Actually I hadn't known that. But I knew how Kevin knew it.

"Come on, he finally got fired," one of the other boys said.

"Yeah, pay up, Lynch," Jimmy De Milio said.

"Forget it, he could be back after vacation," Kevin said. How charming, Kevin had a bet with Jimmy about Mr. P getting fired.

"Look, this is not a topic for discussion," Ms. Sivack said. "There are all kinds of reasons a teacher's out for a week. Mr. Padovano may have very sanely decided he couldn't look at ninth-graders for one more day and started his spring vacation a week early. Now, he wants you in study groups for the chapter on Mediterranean Europe, and then you're to work on the project you started last week, on creating new countries. He left some fact sheets for anyone who was absent Thursday and Friday. I want you in your study groups right now, and get your books open to chapter sixteen."

After class Holly and I zoomed out to the buses and found Mr. Covello in the exact spot where he stands every day pretending he can't wait until he sees our bright shiny faces again tomorrow morning. "Where's Mr. Padovano?" we demanded.

"He's taking a little time off," Mr. Covello said blandly.

"Did you fire him?" Holly asked.

"Of course not," he said. "I don't fire teachers. Only the school board can do that."

Holly rolled her eyes impatiently. "Did *they* fire him?"

"Not as far as I know," he said, sounding totally untrustworthy.

I was really nervous until Holly called after supper and said her mom had found out that the school board hadn't taken any action on Mr. P. "Mom says they might, if someone complaining about him appeared before the board, but no one did at their last meeting, and the mail's running about two-to-one in favor of Mr. P, so they're not gonna do anything on their own," Holly said. "If no one makes a formal complaint at their April meeting, the whole thing's probably gonna fizzle out."

That sounded like pretty good news, which we spread around campus as fast as we could short of hijacking the P.A. system, but it didn't explain why Mr. P wasn't at school. I tried to get his phone number from directory assistance, but it wasn't listed. We were confused.

On Thursday afternoon, we were doing these projects where Mr. P had given us some facts about the location, terrain, climate, and history of a mythical country, and we were supposed to give it a name and make up what its government and society were like now. We were allowed to team up with whoever we wanted for this project, so Holly, Rachel, Sheila, and I were working together. At five to three, Ms. Sivack told us to get finished and clean up the room, and in the classroom chatter I heard Jimmy De Milio, who was working, or I should say not working, in the group next to ours, say to Kevin, "Hey, Lynch, when am I gonna see some money?"

"It ain't over till it's over, De Milio. The guy isn't fired."

"That doesn't mean he's coming back. The pick was Padovano's last day, no matter why he left, and I had last Friday."

"Well, I'm not gonna pay up now. What if he's back after vacation?"

"Wait a minute," I said to Kevin. "You have a pool on when Mr. P's last day is gonna be?"

"Yeah," Kevin said. "I had the Tuesday after that Nerd-Stars reception. Forgot that the school'd put us on display at that B.S. election assembly and he'd stick around for that."

"That's disgusting," Holly said.

"Actually, I wanted to make it a three-way pick: last day, fired or quit, homo or straight. That's a little too sophisticated for this crowd, though, and I don't think there's anybody left who doesn't think the guy's a faggot."

"You really stink," I said hotly. "I would think you of all people would be a little more sensitive to what Mr. P's been going through, considering everything he's done for you, and your brother and all."

Kevin immediately went purple and I looked away from him; I hadn't meant to mention his brother in front of people that way. "What about his brother?"

159

Rachel asked. Holly's eyes got wider and her mouth fell open. I knew she was picturing Kevin's brother, remembering how he looked at the All-Stars—and she realized exactly what I meant.

And after a few seconds, so did a few other people. "Hey, Lynch, your brother's a faggot?" Jimmy asked.

Kevin jumped up so fast that he smashed Jimmy's fingers between their desks. "Ow!" Jimmy screamed. Kevin grabbed his books and ran out of the room as Ms. Sivack yelled, "What happened?" and six kids ran to the door to see where Kevin went. In all the pandemonium, you could just barely hear him pounding his books against one of the lockers. Ms. Sivack went over to Jimmy to see if he was okay, and then the bell rang, and by the time we got into the hall, Kevin was gone.

I went home with Holly that day, called my mother and told her we were working on a project, asked her to pick me up at six. What I really wanted to do was sleep over at Holly's and ride to school on her bus Friday, but Mom won't let me sleep over at anyone's house on a school night. As it turned out, I didn't have to worry about Kevin terrorizing me on the bus. Like Mr. P, he got an early start on his vacation.

Spring break was pretty uneventful. Unlike during Christmas vacation, I slept late every day. Bubbie took Kim and me to a play in the city, which she does every year, and we had a great time. The coolest thing was when Daddy took all of us to opening day of the season at Yankee Stadium. I really like baseball, and Mom is a total Yankee fanatic. She was so excited about going to opening day that she forgot to complain about what a crummy neighborhood Yankee Stadium is in.

The Sunday before we went back to school, a bunch of us went over to Rachel's house, to hang out and prove to her that we were still her friends even though she hadn't been in the All-Stars.

We started talking about who was going to run for Outstanding Girl and Outstanding Boy of the Year. A few years ago the school quit having the two kids with the highest grade point averages speak at ninth-grade graduation and changed it so the teachers nominate about five boys and five girls as the top students in the class. They're supposed to have high grades but also be involved in different school activities and show a lot of school spirit, which lets out most of your major nerds. Then the ninth-graders elect one boy and one girl from the list, usually some student-council types. We decided Holly would definitely be nominated for Outstanding Girl because all her teachers adore her, but Felicia Rim or Heather Rubin would get elected because they've been totally popular since seventh grade.

Rachel ended up giving an informal guitar concert because Holly asked her how her lessons were going, and we all started encouraging her to play. She'd learned a lot of chords and actually was pretty good for only three months of lessons. We made up and sang new words to all the hit songs on the radio, including one for Kevin called "Human Cannonball" and one for Heather Rubin called "I'm a Student Body."

On Monday morning, Kevin wasn't on the bus again, and three seconds after I got to school, I knew why.

Taped to every door and along every wall were dozens of identical Day-Glo green campaign posters, the size of two pieces of notebook paper. Each one had a drawing of Baby Huey, just as goofy as in the comic books but wearing glasses and holding an All-Stars trophy. And each one said, in big black letters,

JANICE GREEN FOR
OUTSTANDING DUCK.

❧ *19* ☙

For a minute or two I just stood in the middle of the hall, staring one way and the other in horror. How I Spent My Spring Vacation, by Kevin Lynch.

Then I heard Holly's voice behind me, "Jan, who did this?"

"Who do you think?" I said.

"What an incredible pig," she said. "How could he have gotten in?"

"I don't know," I said. "He must've sneaked in real early. Maybe one of the custodians left a door open."

Kids were yelling things like "Hey, Green, looks just like you," and going "quack, quack." It was just like sixth grade again.

"Are they all over school?" Holly asked.

"I don't know, I haven't looked," I said. We ran out to the quad behind the main building. The posters were everywhere: tacked onto the portable classrooms, taped to every post and concrete wall. We ran back inside and down the hall to the cafeteria. Day-Glo green every five feet, all around the lunchroom.

I started to cry, and Holly sat me down on the steps next to the cafeteria. "They must be upstairs too; they're everywhere," I sobbed. "We have to take them down!"

Rachel and Sheila came running up to us. "Who did this?" Rachel asked.

"Kevin Lynch," I said.

"Why?" Rachel said.

"Remember when Kevin went nuts in Mr. P's class?" Holly said. "He's trying to get Janice for what she said about his brother before vacation." Without saying a word, Sheila started taking the posters off the walls around the cafeteria entrance and the steps.

"Oh, right," Rachel said. "Are these around the whole school?"

"Yes," Holly said disgustedly.

"Help me take them down," I moaned.

"We don't have time before class," Rachel said.

"Let's go to the office," Holly said. "You should tell them who did this."

"I don't want to be a squealer," I said. "I didn't mean to say anything about Kevin's brother, and telling on him would just make it worse."

"Well, maybe they'll get someone to take them down right away," Holly said. "Come on, let's try to get it done during period one."

Rachel and Sheila went to class, and Holly and I took a poster and went into the main office just as the principal came in from the bus area. "Mr. Covello," I said, holding out a poster. "Somebody—"

"Janice Green, I was just about to summon you from

164

class," Mr. Covello said. "What do you know about these posters?"

"I know I want to take them down!" I said.

"Do you know who posted them?" the principal asked.

"No, I don't," I said. "Does that really matter? I just want to get rid of them."

"Couldn't we pull them down?" Holly asked. "It won't take very long."

Mr. Covello gave me a very hard look, and then he glanced at his watch.

"I'm afraid you don't have time before class," he said. "It's almost eight. Maybe your period-four teacher will excuse you a few minutes early."

"I can't wait till lunchtime!" I said. "The longer they're up, the more people see them! Can you get anybody to take them down?"

"Janice, my staff has better things to do than to go around looking for posters."

"You don't have to look for them, they're everywhere!" I said.

"I'm sorry, you'll have to wait till lunchtime. I can't disrupt school activities just because you have a problem," Mr. Covello said. "Now hurry up to class, or you're both going to get tardy slips."

He went into his office, and we stepped back into the hall. All I could see was Day-Glo green. "What are you going to do?" Holly asked.

"I can't leave them up till lunchtime," I said.

"Maybe if you ask Ms. Zaiman, she'll excuse you from class."

"I can't go to class while those posters are up," I said, crying again. "I can't face anybody."

We were outside the counseling office. "Wait, maybe Ms. Hoxley can get you excused," Holly said. She pulled me into the office just as the tardy bell rang and took me to Ms. Hoxley's little cubicle.

Ms. Hoxley was writing a summons from class for some kid, but she looked up when Holly dragged me into her office. "Ms. Hoxley, Janice has a big problem," Holly said.

"I can see that, and I can guess what it is," Ms. Hoxley said. "How can I help you?" We told her what the principal had said and asked her to get us out of class so we could take down the posters. "I would, except for one thing," she said. "If Mr. Covello sees you taking down the posters and finds out I gave you permission, I'll be in trouble for going against his instructions." Gee, what a risk taker. Ms. Hoxley thought for a second. "Why don't you call your mother?" she said. "If she calls Mr. Covello, I'm sure he'll excuse you right away." That's it, Ms. Hoxley, make sure your rear end's covered.

"I don't know," I said. I was afraid Mom would say something like, "Well, if you dressed a little nicer, people wouldn't make fun of you."

"That's the best I can do," Ms. Hoxley said.

I looked at Holly, who gave me a nothing-to-lose kind of face. I shrugged and picked up the phone. When Mom answered, I said, "Mom, it's me. Somebody put up posters about me as a joke all over school. Could you call the principal and ask him to let me take them down right away?"

Mom didn't sound quite awake. "Wait a minute, Janice, *what* happened?"

"Somebody put up these really mean posters, with my name on them, all over school. Everybody's laughing at me, and the principal won't let me take them down until lunchtime. Can you—"

"I'll be right there," she said. "Where are you?"

I told her, and she hung up. "She said she's coming here right now," I said.

"Oh," Ms. Hoxley said. "In that case, why don't you just stay here and wait for her? I'll send a note to your teacher to mark you present."

"Can Holly stay too?" I asked.

"My mom's left for work, but if you call her office later, I'm sure she'll tell Mr. Covello it was okay," Holly said.

"That's fine," Ms. Hoxley said. She sent a service worker to tell Ms. Zaiman that we were excused.

My mother got there in fourteen minutes. She wasn't wearing makeup, and she normally puts on makeup just to go to the supermarket. Her hair was barely combed, and she was wearing some really ratty jeans and a sweatshirt she never ever wears outside the house when she burst into Ms. Hoxley's office. "Where's the principal?" she asked.

Ms. Hoxley pointed across the hall, and Mom went charging out again. I don't know what she said to Mr. Covello, but in five minutes she was back, a lot calmer, with Mr. Covello, who was smiling very weirdly. "Ms. Hoxley, I think Janice will be able to take down those posters before homeroom if her mother and Holly give her a hand."

"Come on, girls," Mom said.

167

We went through the school like a tornado for the rest of period one, tearing down the posters in handfuls. When we got to the gym, it didn't have any posters, but several of the kids started going "quack, quack" as soon as they saw me. We asked the P.E. teacher if we could go into the locker rooms and check for posters. "I took 'em down in here and in the girls' locker room," she said. "It seemed like the appropriate thing to do, if you know what I mean."

"Thanks," I said gratefully.

"I hear a lot of people who are dying to run serious laps," the teacher said loudly, and the class got quiet right away. "Um, I haven't been in the boys' locker room—just let me send someone in to make sure it's all clear." She ushered us to the door of the locker room and sent a boy in to make sure we wouldn't catch some kid in his jockstrap. Then we went in, and the posters were taped on practically every locker. They were even in the bathroom stalls. I started to cry again.

"I don't understand," Mom said. "Do you know who did this?"

"Yeah, and I know why, but I'm not gonna tell," I said. "I just want to make it go away."

"The person who did this had a reason?" Mom asked.

"Yes, but it's between me and that person," I said. "I'll deal with it, okay?"

For once, Mom let it go. "Okay," she said.

We had the campus cleared by the time the bell rang for homeroom. Mom had a thick roll of green posters under her arm. "I'll throw these out somewhere away from school," she said.

"Thanks, Mom," I said.

"Thanks for helping us, Holly," Mom said. "Janice, do you want to come home with me?"

"No, thanks," I said. "I'll be okay."

"All right, if you're sure," she said. "I'll be home if you need me."

Things got better as soon as the posters were gone. A few kids still quacked when they saw me, and Heather made some snide remark about how she was glad I wasn't running for Outstanding Girl because I'd just be too much competition, but nothing else majorly disastrous happened. My science and Spanish teachers asked me how I was doing, like they wanted to make sure I was okay, and when Holly and I sat down to eat some lunch, Lee came over with some other kids and sat with us, and Lee said he thought I had a lot of guts.

"Yeah, you do," said Liz Feinberg, the school newspaper editor. "I would have been gone; you wouldn't have seen me till June."

"Me too," another girl said. "My mom never would have helped me like that, either. She just would have taken me home."

I felt a little shaky going into period six, though, because Kevin was there and Mr. P wasn't. The fact that Mr. P was still out made me nervous; if he wasn't sick and he wasn't fired, why wasn't he back from vacation? You could tell just from other kids' faces that they were wondering the same thing. But now I was a little angry with him, too: I could have used Mr. P on my side today, and he wasn't there.

I had every intention of ignoring Kevin, but he wouldn't let me. As soon as I sat down, he boomed out, "How's the campaign going, Green?"

169

Fine, how's your brother? I wanted to answer, but God knows what would have happened if I did. "Where'd you get the idea I was running for office?" I said innocently.

"Hey, it's all over school, or at least it was," he said.

"Well, now it's just over," I said.

"Who knows?" Kevin said. "You might find yourself in the limelight, and I do mean the lime *green* light, again tomorrow."

A chill went down my back, but I tried not to show it. "Gee, you'd think people had better things to do with their time and money."

"Giving someone the attention she deserves is worth any amount of effort," Kevin said, leering.

I didn't really think Kevin would put up more posters, but in case he did, I wanted to make sure everybody knew someone else had a serious mental problem, not me. During class I had an idea, and on my way to the bus, I went up to Mr. Covello. "Could you please read this during homeroom announcements tomorrow?" I asked, handing him a piece of paper.

Mr. Covello read the paper and nodded at it, but then he frowned at me. "I'm not sure I want to start a precedent of reading students' messages over the P.A.," he said.

"Someone told me there might be a repeat of the posters tomorrow," I said. "Don't you think this would counteract them?"

"That's not going to happen again," Mr. Covello said firmly. "I'm advising the custodians to keep the doors closed and watch out for unusual activity."

"Yeah, but it shouldn't have happened today, and if

you read that, it'll make the whole episode go away," I said. "If you won't do it on my behalf, I can have my mom talk to you about it."

"No, I'll read it," Mr. Covello said quickly, putting the paper in his pocket.

At home my mother asked me how things went the rest of the day, and I said fine and thanked her for coming and helping me out. Then I went upstairs to do my homework. A few minutes later Mom came into my room. "I just wanted to make sure you were really okay," she said.

"Yeah, really, I am," I said. "The person who put up the posters threatened to do it again, but Mr. Covello said that wasn't going to happen."

"He told me that too," Mom said. "I hope I didn't embarrass you today."

"No, your being there really helped a lot," I said. "I don't think Holly and I could have gotten the posters down so fast by ourselves."

"I got upset when you told me what had happened, and especially when I saw the posters, because something a little like that happened to me when I was in junior high."

"Really?" I said. "What was it?"

Mom sat on my bed. "Well, it must have been in eighth grade. See, I developed, my chest developed, very early, and by junior high I had huge, um, breasts, the biggest in school."

"You were lucky," I said enviously.

"No, Janice, they were too big. It wasn't so bad in high school, but in junior high it just made people stare at me, and laugh at me. And it made me very shy, and because of that, a lot of kids thought I was kind of stuck up."

"Uh-huh," I said.

"So one day, I was sitting in class, I think English class, and this note was going all over the room, and kids were reading it, and giggling over it, and just barely keeping it away from the teacher. And at some point when it was going from one kid to another, I got it, and it wasn't a note at all. It was a picture of me." I gave a sympathetic *ooh*. "Someone had drawn me sitting at a desk in school with my nose in the air, and big, big breasts like balloons resting on the desk. And kids had written awful things all around the picture. A couple of boys wrote very nasty sexual references—you know, things they wanted to do to me."

"Ooh, Mom, that's awful," I said. I couldn't believe she was telling me this.

"That wasn't even the worst thing," Mom said. "Someone else had written, 'Good thing her boobs aren't the size of her personality.' That hurt the most, because I recognized the handwriting. This very cute boy I liked had written it."

I didn't know what to say. She sounded as if she was reliving the whole thing again. "Mom, I'm sorry," I said after a moment.

"I didn't say anything, just put the picture in my notebook and threw it away later. It wasn't as bad as what happened to you, it was just that one picture, but when I saw it, it was the last class of the day, and a friend told me that people had been passing it around since homeroom. I went home and just cried and cried."

Bubbie would have been at work when she got home, too. "Did you tell Bubbie about it?" I asked.

Mom shook her head. "She'd just been promoted at the store, and she was so wrapped up in the new job and working such long hours that I didn't want to bother her with it."

"You must've felt pretty lonely that day," I said.

"I got over it," Mom said. "I just wanted you to know that I know how it feels when people make fun of you because of how you look. Maybe that's why I always want you and your sister to look as nice as you can."

"Yeah, maybe."

"Well, I'll let you get to your homework," she said, getting up. She hesitated by the door. "Any word about Mr. Padovano?"

I shook my head. "Why do you ask?"

She shrugged. "I know you kids miss him."

The next morning, Mr. Covello read my announcement over the P.A.: "Janice Green wishes to announce that she is not a candidate for graduation speaker, but she would like to thank the supporters who worked so hard on her behalf, and she urges all students to make an informed decision for Outstanding Girl and Boy."

Only a couple of kids in my homeroom quacked, and I didn't even care, because by homeroom the news was all over school: Mr. P was back.

❧ 20 ☙

We burst into Mr. P's classroom period six with a collective "WHERE WERE YOU?"

"We thought you were fired!"

"We thought you had AIDS!"

"We thought you quit!"

"We thought you got killed!"

Mr. P waited till we all stopped yelling. "I went to Europe."

That just set us off again. "You WHAT?" we screamed.

"Italy, mostly," he said. "We've spent so much time this year talking about our roots, I thought I'd go check out some of mine. As soon as I get the slides back, I'll show you were I went."

"Why didn't you tell us you were just going on vacation?" Patty Zymont asked. "We were worried!"

"To be perfectly honest, I wasn't sure I'd be coming back," Mr. P said.

"Did you think you were gonna get fired?" Rachel asked.

"No, by the time I took off, I was pretty much assured that all that business had blown over, thanks in part to the efforts of some very nice people I know," he said, smiling at Holly and me and a few others in the class. "I just wasn't sure I was coming back."

"You were thinking of quitting?" I asked in disbelief. "Just never coming back and never telling us why?"

"Well, when you put it that way, Janice, it seems like a pretty crummy thing to do," Mr. P said. "I guess that's why I didn't do it."

"It's a pretty crummy thing to even think about doing," I said hotly.

Patty raised her hand. "Mr. P, I think I speak for *most* of us in this room and maybe at school when I say that we don't care if, I mean, what you are or how you live, because you're a great teacher and we're just glad you're back." There was a little chorus of *yeah*s, and about half the class started clapping.

Mr. P smiled a little crookedly. "Well, Patty, I'm going to take that statement in the spirit in which I'm sure you meant it and say thank you. Now I've got a lot of catching up to do, and I need your cooperation. I'm hoping you got up to chapter eighteen in the text—"

Jason Baron interrupted him. "So, come on, Mr. P, you can tell us now, are you gay or what?"

Dead silence. "Excuse me?" Mr. P said.

Jason looked uncomfortable, since most of the girls in the room were looking at him like, you dork, but he held his ground. "I mean nobody cares anymore, so you can tell us."

"Obviously *you* care, or you wouldn't ask," Holly said contemptuously.

Mr. P sighed. "Jason, my private life wasn't any of your business last fall or last month, and it's none of your business now, any more than Ms. Zaiman's private life is any of your business, or Mr. Covello's, or Mr. Geiger's."

"Geiger doesn't have a private life," one of the boys said.

"I will tell you this much, though," Mr. P said. Everybody leaned forward. Mr. P filled his voice with drama. "You want to know if I'm gay, right? Well, there may be a one-in-ten chance that I am."

Half the kids in the class sucked in their breath as if Mr. P had made some big confession. "You are? I mean, there is?" Jason asked.

I couldn't stand it. "It's the same chance *you're* gay, you doofus," I said to Jason. "In any big group of people, somebody's gonna be gay."

Jason went red. "Spoken like a future dyke, Baby Huey," he said.

To my surprise, Kevin muttered. "Baron, you're an idiot."

"That's enough," Mr. P snapped. "Everybody quiet. Janice is correct. A certain percentage of the population is gay or lesbian. It may be one or two in every hundred, or it may be as high as ten percent; nobody's really sure. But whatever the percentage is, it's a lot of people. That may not mean much to you now, but what it does mean is that someday, sooner or later, someone close to you is going to turn out to be gay. It could be a friend, a teacher, a relative." Almost every kid in the class turned his or her face toward Kevin except Jimmy De Milio, who still had a couple of bandaged fingers, and me. After a moment I turned my head just enough to see Kevin out of the corner of my eye. He was sitting calmly, his arms folded like usual, looking straight ahead at Mr. P. "Trust me on this one: Next week, next year, ten, twenty years from now, someone you care about is going to tell you he or she is gay, and you're either going to realize that it doesn't matter, it's still the same person, you still care about him or her—or you're going to reject that person, which means you will have lost someone you care about."

Everybody let that sink in. "That ends any discussion I want to have in this classroom about sexual orientation," Mr. P said. "Now some responsible person, I don't care who, is going to bring me up to date on where you left off in the textbook, and I'm going to want an update from each project group on where you are."

When class was over, Mr. P came over to me as I loaded my backpack. "I heard you had a pretty awful experience yesterday," he said.

"Yeah," I said briefly.

"I also heard you handled it well," he said. "I was very impressed by your announcement in homeroom."

"Thanks," I said. "I got a lot of moral support from friends, you know, people who happened to be at school yesterday."

"Uh-huh," Mr. P said. "Your nemesis seems to have come through without ill effects."

He meant Kevin. "How do you know all this? Were teachers faxing you bulletins or something?"

"Hey, this was five minutes' chat in the faculty

lunchroom," he said. "Teachers lead very boring lives. Whom do you think we gossip about?"

"Touché, Mr. P.," I said, picking up my backpack. "I gotta catch my bus." I had a couple of questions for my nemesis.

"Hey, Huey, wake up, you're home," Kevin yelled when we got to my bus stop and I didn't get off.

"I've got somewhere else to go," I called back. He scowled at me.

I waited for Kevin's stop and got off after him. He strode as fast as he could toward his house, and I had to run to keep up. "Lynch, I want to talk to you," I gasped.

"Got nothing to talk about," he said.

"Look, I'm sorry I said anything about your brother. I didn't mean to, really. You were being such a pig, and it just came out."

"Yeah, that's what they call it, coming out. Look, Huey, I accept your apology. Run along like a good little girl."

We were getting close to his house, and I was determined to keep him outside until he told me what I wanted to know. "Lynch, I don't get it. How can you be so mean about gay people when your brother is gay?"

"In the words of Saint Padovano, it's none of your business."

"I want to understand," I pleaded. "I mean he seems like a neat guy, and you obviously care about him, so how can you go around using words like *homo* and *faggot?*"

Kevin turned up his driveway. "Have a nice day, Huey," he said.

Don't piss me off, you fat creep. "No!" I yelled, running in front of him. "You don't get away that easy! Everybody's gonna forget about your brother, but you made sure nobody forgets Baby Huey! You could be doing detention from now till the end of time, but I didn't squeal! You owe me!" He stood there, glowering at me, but he didn't move. "I just want to understand," I said. "If you hate gays so much, why do you hang out with your brother? Why is it okay for him to be gay and not Mr. P?"

He opened his mouth as if he were going to answer, then brushed past me. "Go ahead and tell them about the posters, I don't care."

I ran right behind him and grabbed his arm so hard that he spun around. "No!" I screamed. "Answer me! Why is it okay for your brother to be gay and not anybody else?"

"It's not okay!" he yelled. "My brother's a faggot! He got fired from two jobs because he's a faggot! My grandparents won't talk to him because he's a faggot! He's gonna die because he's a faggot!" He had backed me into the garage door of his house. "There's your answer, Green: It's not okay! You happy now?"

"Wow," I said. "I'm sorry. I'm really sorry."

"I don't need your sympathy," Kevin said, turning away.

"Is he scared?" *Are you scared?* I wanted to ask.

"I don't know. Probably. Look, Green, I told you what you wanted to know, didn't I? Get lost."

A thought hit me. "You know, your brother's not sick because he's gay," I said.

That got his attention. "What?" he said impatiently.

"He's got AIDS, right?"

"Yeah," Kevin said.

"Then he's sick because he has AIDS, not because he's gay," I said. "You don't have to be gay to get AIDS."

"No, but it helps," he said sullenly. "Half his faggot buddies are dead and the rest are just waiting. Ask Padovano what it's like to have one foot in the grave and the other on a banana peel."

"No, he's . . ." I realized that it wasn't going to make Kevin feel any better to know that Mr. P was okay. "I'm sorry," I said. "You're right, you told me what I wanted to know. I still think you're the creep of the century for putting up those posters, but I understand why you were so mad."

"Fine," Kevin said, going up his front steps. "Look, if it's any consolation, those posters cost a fortune, and I don't think it was worth it. I thought they'd stay up until at least lunchtime, and I expected you to get a lot more upset."

"Gee, thanks for telling me," I said with just a hint of sarcasm. Coming from Kevin, that was like a round of applause. "And if it's any consolation to *you*, I was really, really hurt."

"Well . . . good," he said, almost smiling, "Later, Green."

"Okay, once again, the written portion of your project is due on Monday," Mr. P called into the late-

Friday chatter. "Patty, one page on clothing is more than enough; Kevin, please keep in mind that cultural life goes beyond air guitar; Bobby, I really think a five-house legislature is excessive. Remember, oral reports from each group start Tuesday, so keep in touch with your teammates over the weekend."

The bell rang and everybody raced out except a few kids who had questions about their projects. When I was about to leave, Mr. P stopped talking to Bobby Kirschbaum and said, "Janice, wait, I want you to read something." I went over to his desk, and he gave me a folded-up newspaper clipping.

Mr. P is always giving kids stuff he cuts out of the paper, so I just unfolded it and started to read, but when I saw what it was about, I went back to my desk and sat down. The headline read, *Looking Forward to Coming Out*. There was no byline, and a note under the headline said that the writer was withholding his name to protect his current and future jobs as a teacher.

The article was about everything Mr. P had been through since December: having his car and his class-room door vandalized, the rumors and how they affected his teaching, feeling as if the school administration didn't support him enough, the parents' meeting, the weeks of wondering whether he'd be fired. He wrote about how, after years of hugging kids and slapping high fives with them and holding their hands when they were upset, now there were only a few he felt he could even pat on the shoulder to say "good work." He wrote about Kevin, how if he were able to tell Kevin he was gay, he might be able to help him work out the anger he felt about his brother's being sick. He said he wanted his students to know he was gay not because he wanted them to be gay but because he wanted them to know it was okay to be different in any way, not just sexually, but physically or ethnically or any other way. And he wrote that although his job probably wasn't at risk, he would leave his current school if he could find a position in a district where being gay was no big deal.

When I finished reading the article, the other kids were gone, I was crying, and the buses were pulling away. "Oh, no, there goes my bus," I moaned.

Mr. P was stuffing papers in his briefcase. "Padovano's Taxi, at your service," he said, smiling.

It was nice to ride in Mr. P's car again. "Where was that article printed?" I asked.

"Union newspaper," he said. "I'm thinking of sending it to one of the national teachers' magazines. Heck, I may see if *Newsweek*'ll take it."

"That'd be so cool," I said. "Are you really gonna leave West River?"

"I've sent out résumés to other districts," he said. "New York City is probably the only place around here where they really don't care about sexual orientation, but that would involve a big cut in pay. I may be back here if it looks like the anti-gay folks can't do more than blow a little hot air and if the district will back me up if they do. But this year has taught me a lot, Janice. I thought if I was a good enough teacher, it wouldn't matter if people knew I was gay. Well, guess again." I nodded sadly. "And I found out that being in the closet bothers me more than I thought it did. Sooner or later,

I'm gonna have to come out no matter what the consequences."

"Were you really thinking about not coming back from your vacation?"

"We weren't in a big hurry to come home from Europe, that's for sure. No, I was pretty sure I could finish out the school year. I've never liked wimps very much. They make lousy role models."

"Well, everybody's glad you're back. I think even Kevin's glad."

"You think so? That's one angry kid. As you well know."

I nodded again. "I made him tell me why he could be so mean to you and say nasty things about gay people when he cared so much about someone who's gay."

"Oh, I didn't find that hard to understand at all. The second I met Kevin's brother at the All-Stars, everything fell into place: his attitude, why he didn't want to join the All-Stars, why he painted my car, everything."

What? "You knew he painted your car?" I yelled.

"Yeah, sure, he told me a few days later. He finished paying me back for the paint job around the end of January."

"But he stayed with the All-Stars," I said, half to myself.

"Yeah," Mr. P said. "And since Kevin is the kind of kid who does exactly as he pleases, I have the feeling he enjoyed being on the team. Not that you'd ever get him to admit that."

"But what's his problem with you being gay?"

"Janice, he isn't mad at me for being gay," Mr. P said. "He's mad at me for being gay and *healthy*. I don't know how much longer his brother's going to be around, but it obviously won't be forever. Meanwhile, he sees me at school every day—I don't know how he figured out I'm gay, he picked it up somehow—and I'm happy, healthy, working, not a worry in the world that he can see. He's angry at his brother, and I've never so much as said boo to him, but what's he going to do, yell at his brother for being sick? I'm a convenient and, to him, appropriate target for his anger."

"It still isn't very nice," I said.

"Neither is losing someone you love," Mr. P said. "Don't worry, Janice. I think Kevin learned a lot this year too, and I don't mean the principal products of Bolivia."

"You don't think *Kevin's* gay, do you?" I asked.

Mr. P laughed so hard he almost choked. "Are you kidding? He spends most of every period six staring at girls. When I see drool collect in the corner of his mouth, I ask him a question just to snap him out of it. He's got a huge crush on Holly."

"Oh, yeah," I said, remembering the way he'd looked at Holly when she was helping him with math—and the magazine we'd found in his bed. "Do you think I'm gay? I'm not attracted to any of the boys I know. In fact, I think most of them are disgusting."

"What about boys you don't know?" Mr. P asked. "You know, like actors, or some guy you see on the street?"

I thought for a second. "I guess I might think, oh, he's cute, but not about him touching me or anything."

"Hmmmm," Mr. P said. "Are you attracted to other girls?"

184

"Like sexually?" I said. I tried to imagine *that*.

"Uh-uh. Definitely not."

"In other words, you don't feel physically attracted by anyone of either sex?"

"No, I guess not. Not yet, anyway."

"And you're how old?"

"I was fourteen in December."

"Well, give it a little more time," Mr. P said. "You should know any minute now."

❧ 21 ❧

It was warm for the end of April, and I almost missed the bus because it took me forever to convince Mom it was silly for me to take a jacket when it was going to be eighty degrees in about five minutes.

I raced onto the bus just as the driver was reaching for the door handle, pushed my glasses up my nose, and plopped down about halfway back. The trees were a soft, fuzzy green, and everybody's rhododendron bushes were blooming. I took *The Catcher in the Rye*, which Mr. P had lent me, out of my backpack and started reading. It was great. The main character reminded me a little of Kevin, only cuter. Maybe I'd recommend it to him when I was done.

"Hey, lardass!" Kevin yelled from the back. Well, maybe I wouldn't.

I looked around. "What is it, Your Blubberosity?" I said.

"Is Padavano giving us a test today?"

"Yeah."

186

"What on?"

"Central America."

"Oh, yeah," he said. I don't know why he bothered asking. He was going to ace the test. He aced all of Mr. P's tests.

A few minutes later I heard Kevin lumber up the aisle and thud into the seat behind me. "Oh, *The Catcher*," he said. "I bet you have a big old crush on Holden C, don'tcha, Green?" Grrr. Sometimes I think the only book Kevin hasn't read is *The Baby-Sitters Club Goes to a Disco*. "Don't worry, you'll get over it after he gets drunk and breaks his sister's record," he added.

"Do you *mind?*" I said. "I'd like to find out what happens without any help from you."

"Sure," he said. "But I'm gonna have to make you a reading list. That stuff Padovano gives you isn't gonna help you be less of a social retard. You need some cooler role models."

"Like you, I suppose," I said as sarcastically as I could.

"You could do worse," Kevin said, getting up.

He went back to the rear of the bus, and for a moment I had a pleasant vision of the emergency door springing open and Kevin falling under the wheels of a truck. But then I'd never get that reading list.

ABOUT THE AUTHOR

Author ELLEN JAFFE MCCLAIN says: "In writing this story, I wanted to show that kids, whether they know it or not, have gay men and lesbians in their lives as teachers, friends, and relatives—and that being gay is just part of who those important people are. By extension, I wanted to show that there's nothing wrong with being 'different' in *any* way."

The author has written many articles for national magazines and is at work on her first nonfiction book. For more than ten years, she has taught junior and senior high school English in Los Angeles, where she lives with her husband, Spencer Gill.